The Controlled Burn

The Controlled Burn

-or-

I'm not thinking

A Novel

TOM KUHAR

Wiesbaden V Printing

FIRST WIESBADEN V EDITION, JULY 2017

Cover design by Bridget E. Sheffler

ISBN: 0692870598
ISBN 13: 9780692870594

First edition

PROLOGUE

What this is is not a story. It's not a fable or a parable and it definitely has no meaning or moral voice to it.

Redeeming social value? Not here, brother.

It won't make you feel better about yourself and it won't help grow hair and you're still overweight. Trust me.

There's no subliminal messages, there's no secret meaning, there's definitely no real point.

There are no portrayals of heroic measures. This isn't what English teachers call a myth or an epic or a dramatization of anything. This shouldn't even be in a classroom, if you get where I'm coming from.

What it is is the part of you that looks at a car wreck on the highway, staring stupidly at the twisted metal and hanging limbs. It's the part of you that tries to recreate the crime scene. Whose car hit whose and that sort of stuff. By the skid marks he must have been going 75 miles per hour.

What it is is the way that every year there are less and less World War II vets meeting at their annual conventions. Less people reliving the Battle of the Bulge. The flag raising at Iwo Jima. Maneuvers in North Africa. The fire bombing of Dresden. The war is long over, but they all wind up casualties in the end.

What it is is the old woman who habitually reads the obituaries to see which of her high school classmates she's managed to outlive.

Because the simple fact is every one who chooses to love you will one day not care about you at all. Every ex-girlfriend, every best friend since the sixth grade, every first kiss, they all go away.

And just where is the first girl you kissed? See?

Really, this is more like addition through subtraction than anything else.

What it is is the fact that people will bury an empty coffin if they can't find the body to put in there.

Because if you're a midget, no matter how old you get, there's for sure no way you're getting on those big loop the loop roller coasters.

What it is is the place in your head that doesn't so much care about life after death but really wants to catch *Modern Family*. Have good seats to the game. A table at that trendy restaurant or tickets to the chic art exhibit by that gay guy you've never heard of.

Because no matter what medicine says, you're going to die anyway. Every breath is one less. In the big picture, you're only 175 pounds for the Earth to recycle. Every single time you wake up to a beautiful day with a wide blue sky and all that, well, you failed the one damn thing you were put here to do.

What I'm trying to say is it's all inevitable.

Birth- end of the beginning or beginning of the end, you decide.

It's going to happen whether you care or not. It's not like you can stop it. No, really. You are going to die.

Because people only love you due to a chemical reaction. Lust is just something in the bloodstream. Passion is an endorphin overdose. No lie.

What this is is the bedroom of some kid who died in high school, and now twenty years later, his room has remained untouched. His Playboys are still under his bed, the Kathy Ireland poster is still over his desk. His mother still washes the sheets every week, and yes, there's even the model airplane hanging from the ceiling by fishing line.

Because change may be a constant but it doesn't always happen.

What this is is four seconds before impact. Everyone always tells you to relax when you hit, but you can put your faith in the fact you'll forget that one when the asphalt comes up screaming at you. What this is is terminal velocity.

This isn't as much "turn the other cheek" as it is "eye for an eye, tooth for a tooth."

What this is is the complete opposite of *Oprah's Book Club*.

So don't worry. Don't try to learn things you don't need. Molecular physics won't beat cancer, believe me. Algebra may tell you what the value of $x+5$ is, but it won't do a thing to a major stroke. Don't get me started on how Russian literature is worthless during a seizure.

And please don't look too deep at this. Just name one person saved by philosophy or lofty morality or ethical superiority.

Because even Einstein has wasted away by now. Seriously.

What this is is culmination. End product. Final result. Grand finale. The climax.

What it is is everything coming together.

1

Sadly, as much as I had hoped that a greasy breakfast bagel from Dunkin' Donuts would ease my hangover, this did not prove true. Sadly, staring at my computer screen only seemed to suck my energy, my soul, my very fucking essence, and now my headache crept deeper, past my eyes, past my temples surrounding my brain. Sadly, I just threw up in my wastebasket.

Maybe I am getting older but I used to be able to drink like this every day and not feel a damn thing. No puking, nothing. Now, I feel like America runs on Chuckin'. Christ, the wastebasket reeks of bile and Stoli. This is not good. My fiancée, Monica, is due at my office any minute now for lunch and some last minute planning for the wedding. It is planned for July 17. Today is July 9. We have just 8 days until we are to be united to each other, husband and wife, now until the end of eternity. I just threw up again.

It's a real pain in the ass to vomit AND try to keep your $225 silk tie out of the wastebasket.

I need a nap bad. There's only so much I can expect the girls in the make-up department to do. I need to look healthy, not like a wax dummy.

I just arrived back in my office from cleaning the wastebasket out in the janitor's sink at the end of the hall and switching it with Paul's wastebasket. They are the same color and size and Paul is a fucking idiot anyway. There's no such thing as an intelligent sportscaster, let me tell you.

"Why are you carrying that trashcan around for dear life, honey?" Monica had arrived unseen and was sitting at my desk. "And what is that smell?"

"Oh. Just trying to find some trash bags that fit is all. Can't find one. It's like the Dark Ages or something. I think someone down the hall is burning incense. "Tapioca Jambalaya" or something. Who knows? Ready?"

We walked down the hall, hand in hand as usual. We decided to eat at the Mexican place around the corner, Don Cervaza's. It was, at best, an odd ride over. Monica looked as if she had something to say but knew I was mired in the self-pity of a hangover. Her gaze was half unapproving, half remorse for my sloven position. I couldn't keep my eyes open. The sunlight was assaulting me, bleaching my cones and rods. OK, I really need to throw up again. Restrain, restrain, restrain, wait until we get to the restaurant.

As we walked up to the doors, I opened a door gently for Monica, and then entered after her. The server, some strung out surfer, seated us next to an old fountain filled with pennies. I pulled Monica's seat out so she could be seated, then quietly turned towards the restrooms.

They were around the corner, past the bar (I couldn't even look), to the right. It was a serene powder blue, the color of a perfect summer's day's sky, I guess. I caught sight of myself, alone, 29, about to be married, hair messed up, tie askew, hungover like a senior after the prom. What a sight. Pathetic.

Then I threw up, a third time, in the middle sink.

■ ■ ■

My lovely fiancée greeted me as I returned to the table. "Feeling better, honey?"

I'm not thinking *Hungover like Hiroshima* but I couldn't blame you if you were.

"Indeed, sweetheart. What did you order?"

"For me I got the fajita combo with chili con carne. You're getting the Below the Border special. No chili."

"*No* chili? What?" Chili is a staple of my Mexican eating. It is the side dish of choice for any Mexican dish. Any dish. Chili has no ethnic predispositions or conditions attached to it. Monica knows this, has known this, will know this forever.

"No chili. It gives you gas."

"And?"

"And, you're not eating chili and then sleeping next to me tonight. And you're sleeping next to me tonight." Can't argue with that logic.

I was in no mood to argue, anyway. Besides, chili could have proven a disastrous call, with all the recent vomiting. I sat pensively, motionlessly, becoming one with the chair. It was a rather nice restaurant, all in all. It looked like a restaurant that Disney might build to stick in the Mexico section of some theme park, only to be inhabited by mechanical cartoons spitting catch phrases and feel-good anesthesia.

I can just see the talking dog (who of course walks upright), wearing tie die and loud shorts telling me all about recycling. There's the bird, with coloring I've never found in an Audubon field guide, spouting all kinds of information about the rapid depletion of the rainforest and other important ecosystems.

The feisty cat and the fluoride in the water. The evil fucking bear that runs the faucet while brushing his teeth.

Eventually I returned to our table and my gaze settled on Monica's more-than-ample cleavage. Damn, I'm a lucky man. I should have noticed this earlier but I was too afraid to make eye contact with her for fear of a dirty look. She was keen on dirty looks as well as digging her nails into your arm when you said something dumb. Her hair was down, delicate locks of hair framing her face. Her eyes seemed full, shining, and blue. Her face was lit up, like that famous picture of Westminster Abbey with the light pouring through the stained glass and her chestnut hair had the sexy sheen to it. Plus her shirt was short and her blouse was tight. What else can you ask for? It's a T&A Matinee.

The food arrived. Monica began to eat, almost ravenously, though in a truly feminine manner. I, on the other hand, picked at my food. I could not eat this... this... food. It had to be the way the cheese was melted over the tiny hard beans. Repulsive.

"Something the matter, babe? You haven't eaten a bite."

"No. I'm fine. Just not hungry is all."

"U-huh. Are *we* hung over today?" Oh, great. Now I'm getting the royal "We". Beautiful. Took her long enough to arrive at her guilt trip destination.

"Just a little. A mild headache. No biggie."

"U-huh. And are we going out again this evening?"

"Ahhh... yeah, yeah I am- with Dennis, Dave, Rob, and Mike. To Skibble's. Won't be out too *too* late, I swear."

Pause. She paused. This is good. She's rethinking. Take your time, sexy. Take. Your. Time.

"You know, you're acting like you're in college again."

"Oh, babe, you knew full well that I was obligated to party down with the guys the week prior to the wedding. They all just want a last night out with me. Old time's sake. You know the deal. This is Premarital 101, babe."

"And they're going to get that night in three days, at your bachelor party." Not this again.

"Ok, but they sort of want just us, the guys from LaSalle. There's going to be over 50 people at my bachelor party. They just want some privacy. Alone time."

"Alone in a crowded bar? She does that pouty eye roll that is sexy as hell when given to others. I'm not others, so it sucks.

"Oh, you get the point. You knew all about this. You didn't have a problem with it three weeks ago when I told you all about it."

She paused again. All right, now just glide her down smooth. No quick moves, just nice and steady, nice and steady. Just glide in the landing.

"God, Monica, I hope you're not going to act like this when we're married."

Fuck. Fuck. Fuck. Fuck.

About face. Retreat. Retrograde motherfucking action.

"What I meant to say, what I *really* meant wasn't that at all, it was more different than that. Wow. I really need to think *before* I speak." My voice withered under a gaze more intense than million supernovas.

A glare. All I got was a red hot, monotonous glare.

2

Monica drops me off back at the office after a pretty quiet drive back. She gives me this half-ass kiss in the cheek when I go to kiss her on the lips. She just moved away like I'm some sort of asshole because I'm going out with the guys.

I would have been more pissed off about this but I was too hungover to say much. I go back to my office and my secretary Megan is sitting there reading a magazine and when I come in, she hides it like I actually care and asks me if I want a cup of coffee, tells me I look like shit. Yeah, well, thanks. And who the fuck reads magazines anymore? We have the god damned internet now.

I need to think of pointless things for her to do from now on. Most of what she does is either making me copies of papers no one needs an extra copy of, or texting her boyfriend on her phone. Maybe even sexting. I should ponder that further. Anyway, he does customer service at some furniture store in the suburbs. He sounds gay to me, but he does have a girl-friend so who knows anymore.

I'm sitting behind my desk when the phone rings. Megan's walking in, so I know she can't answer unless she drops my cup of coffee on the rug. I pick it up and it's a wrong number for Paul so I act like I can't hear them until they hang up.

I grab my coffee, the paper, and head off down the hall. As I walk out, I hear the phone ringing yet again.

I go into the bathroom, and enter the middle stall. I drop my pants and seat myself. To my right, in permanent black marker, it says "PAUL FUCKS LITTLE BOYS". Under it, in blue pen, it says "Fuck you Asshole Cocksucker" in this queer-ass pansy cursive handwriting.

I wonder if it's Paul sticking up for himself. It probably is, but I'm surprised he could even manage to write such profanity. I have no clue how this man is a sportscaster. What a homo. He spends so much time with his personal stylist, it makes me sick. He gets the lead-ins, he gets live camera time, he is the main guy in our stupid little ads. Him. It's his big fucking face on the billboards. What do I get? Jack shit.

That's why I have this black permanent marker. To bring him back to Earth. To be his constant reminder. To be the glass of water thrown in the face of a hysterical woman.

So when he's at his most vulnerable, when his pants are around his knees, that's when he's reminded of the hate someone has for him, some random person. It could be any one on the floor with a key to the restroom.

And he knows they hate him pretty bad. It's the paranoia that kills him.

And with these permanent markers, even if they paint over it, it'll still show through. Two coats, three coats, four coats, it doesn't even matter. Black always shows through.

In the left stall, under two coats of pastel yellow, if you try really hard, you can still read a dirty limerick entitled "Paul's Balls".

Archeologists in Egypt were studying a dig site and deciphered a wall that they claimed changed the face of historical study in regards to Egypt. Did it mention political turmoil, or natural disasters that forced hundreds of thousands of people to starve?

Nope.

Did it shed light on how religion manifested itself in Egypt's educational system?

Nope. It was graffiti.

So I take out the marker, remove the cap, and set out to react to Paul's silly rebuttal.

■ ■ ■

I'm going over the Doppler readout for the Midwest when the producer for the six o'clock show knocks on my door and comes in, even before I can say to.

"Billy, we're having a production meeting in fifteen. We have some big ideas for you."

"What this time? Why do you always have to screw with my shit?"

"Oh, come on- you'll love this. You'll get primo air time, trust me."

Last time "primo air time" meant manning the phones at a PBS fundraiser.

"Because every Thursday from now on, you'll be live from some school in the area. It's a giving-back-to-the-community kind of thing. People eat this shit up."

"No fucking way. I'm not sitting in some germ factory with a bunch of fucking kids. I hate fucking kids. They're walking lymph nodes of infectious, puss-oozing, suppurating disease. I told you, I hate fucking kids."

"No, you *fucking* hate kids, not hate *fucking* kids."

Huh?

"When you say that you hate fucking kids, it sounds like you don't like having sex with kids. Who does? It's a context thing. Grammar. You fucking hate them."

What ever. I don't like kids.

"I think you already said that and thank God we don't pay you to like kids. We pay you to do a live remote each and every week and you're going to do them from a school. Maybe they'll be having a science fair. Maybe they'll be doing some benefit for homeless crack dogs or whatever. Maybe the Virgin Mary will have appeared in the mildew on the grout in the teacher's lounge. I don't care why, I just care that you're there."

I can tell he's not going to budge so I just sit there, trying to look a lot more pissed than I actually am. He realizes his victory and starts to leave my office when he stops, turned around, looks me dead in the eyes and says, "And do me a favor- no rain this weekend. I have a golf tourney this weekend," and walks out.

Like I'm God or something. Like I have some kind of supernatural control over that situation.

It's not even like I'm a meteorologist or some shit. Even then, all I could do I predict the weather, not change it to suit everyone's plans. Every single day of my life, someone tries to get me to do them a favor. Give them the heads up on the weather. Have a buddy's back. Like a simple wave of my hand and it's all sun with low humidity.

Like if I say it on the air, nature is legally bound to do it.

I'm buying fresh Asian pears in the supermarket and this lady wants this Thursday to be nice because it's her kid's school picture day. Another day, some kid that I'm buying my daily soft pretzel (spicy mustard, no salt) from wants a thunder-shower so his Little League gets cancelled. "Make sure there's lightening or else they won't call the game. Gotta be within five miles," he tells me.

All I want to do is pick up my laundry but I have to make sure the rain lets up soon or the field will be too muddy for the marching band to practice and they go for the state title in two weeks time, don't you know?

Megan walks in and tells me its ten minutes until the show. I rub my eyes, check my hair one last time in the mirror, and walk out in to the studio.

3

I was at the bar, Skibble's Fine Establishment, with Dennis and Dave and Rob and Mike. No more hangover. It's amazing what an afternoon nap, a big bowl of pasta, and seven Advil can do sometimes. I am well rested for this new night of bacchanal.

They were talking to me, asking questions, expecting answers. Input, output. Cause and effect. A butterfly flaps his wings in Tokyo and my friends ask me the last time I nailed someone besides Monica. Who opened for Radiohead at that show a few years ago. Have I ever heard from Freddy McManus since graduation.

Something, somewhere deep inside tells my brain it's time to respond.

"This girl, Mandy maybe, I met in a bar. We were together for a week or so."

"Wasn't it some crappy band named Dog Eat Dog or something?

"No, haven't heard from Jerk-off Freddy in years."

"She just said I was being rude, selfish, and immature."

"Yeah, Jimmy Kramer and Paul Martin are going to be there. Ed Walton, too."

"No, the Tigers won the World Series in '84. The Orioles won in '83."

"Don't play any fucking Bruce Springsteen. I want Beatles, Floyd, Alice in Chains, Nirvana, maybe some Zeppelin. No Springsteen crap."

"Uh, tequila, I guess. Cuervo Gold, por favor."

I think I've caught up. There don't seem to be any inquiries pending.

I look up and down the bar, pondering my friends and looking for any other familiar faces. There were none. Just my four college buddies, slowly getting hammered on draft beers and various shots. This was all quite normal anytime any of the five of us got together. When we were at LaSalle in Philadelphia, we partied quite a bit. These are the guys who held my hair out of the toilet when I was puking up SoCo and Pepsi. These are the guys I road tripped with down to the Outer Banks in North Carolina our junior year. Talk about hedonism. Five guys, three days, two kegs. You can do the math.

There just never seems to be enough lighting in bars. You cannot make out exactly what you are looking at, be it a sign, the television, or an attractive woman. Maybe this adds to the faint social escape a bar usually is, but really now- it all leaves you dry. Dry and wanting. Or maybe I am just drunk.

Everybody was finally done asking me those dumb questions about my whatever it was with Monica. One trivial exchange of words and I get ten minutes of that trite "trouble in paradise" bullshit from everyone. Fucking people, man.

Either they had asked all the pertinent questions, everybody was too intoxicated to continue the investigation or a combination therein. They call me a cab which pisses me off because now tomorrow morning I'll need to take a cab to get my car but I deal with it.

4

Alarm clock. Loud. Ringing. Head hurts. Turn off alarm clock, fall back into bed. Asleep again.

Phone ringing. Pick up, mute button. Rings again. Same response. Asleep again.

Monica standing over me. Roll over, try to go back to sleep. No chance.

"It's past one! Why aren't you at work? Why are you still in bed? What in the *world* is going on here?" I can just sense this is going to go poorly. "You know we need to be at the church in forty minutes for a walk through. Father Tim is expecting us."

The thought process resumes. Slowly, the rust and fermented yeast burns off and clears the way for my synapses to fire fire fire.

"I called and said I'd be late for the five o'clock show."

"Oh really? Then why when I called your office, did Megan ask why you weren't in yet, are you sick?"

Uncontrollable laughter. This is hurting but it's so damn funny.

"What the fuck? Are you laughing at me? Are you laughing at *me*?"

I'm not thinking Joe Pesci but I can't blame you if you were.

"…no…no… not you at all… a joke… give me… a minute." She glared at me hard again. Really, it was hard to catch my breath.

"It's not you, babe. It's a joke I heard last night. Funny as shit. Ok, it's like this. There's this guy, he gets a new job and he's told to show up Monday morning at 8 o'clock. So, Monday morning rolls around, the guy calls in saying he's sick and he can't make it in. Well, the boss figures everyone gets sick now and again so he says that's fine, be here tomorrow at 8. The next day, the guy shows up on time and works hard all day. Same for Wednesday and the rest of the week. Next Monday rolls around, again the guy calls in, saying he's sick and can't come in to work. The boss grudgingly says be here tomorrow bright and early. But the rest of the week, he's on time and super productive. But, the third Monday, same call. He's sick and can't make it in. So, Tuesday morning, the guy shows up and the boss calls him into his office and asks him, 'What gives? Every Monday you call in sick. Are you drinking too much? Is it drugs? We can get you help. You're a good worker, I want to work this out.'"

"A guy who's too sick to go to work is that funny?"

"Hold on, there's more, let me finish. So, the guy tells him that's not it at all. It's his sister. 'Sister?' says the boss. 'What the hell do you mean?' So the guy tells her that his sister is in an abusive relationship. 'Every weekend her husband gets all drunk and beats the crap out of her. So, every Monday after he leaves for work she calls me in tears. I go over to console her and one thing leads to another and we end up spending the day having the most passionate, toe curling sex humanly possible.' The boss looks at the guy and says 'That's DISGUSTING!' The guy looks at him and says 'I told you I was sick.'"

"Oh, goodness William, that's horrible. You need help." I can see a smirk in there.

"It's funny. You know it's funny. Laugh, damn you, laugh. Hahafrigginha." She's giggling a little, I'm golden. "Look, let me grab a shower, I got to shower and after Padre Tim, we'll grab a bite. Pick a place." She's giving me a look, but a good look. God, I love this woman. Accepts my faults, forgiving, cooks, hot, the total package.

And then her gaze darkens. Her eyes start to draw shut.

"So, did we *toke* some *reefer* last night?" Suddenly I'm royalty again.

I'm not thinking King William IV but I can't blame you if you were.

"Man, yeah, some. And?"

"Ok. Hmmm. Did we have the nose candy? Did we?"

"Well, yeah, some, a line or two, and… well… yeah." There's not a crisis team skilled enough for this. "Babe, you know it's all going to stop when I say 'I do', you know that. Monica, come on now."

I'm no cokehead. I snort a few lines here and there. No biggie. No shooting up, no addiction. Strictly recreational.

A little on-the-weekend action. I never even buy the stuff, I just chip in. I don't even know the dealer's name. What's the big deal here? Even Cheech was a network star for a minute. We had a president that admitted to toking and another who snorted his way through college and another who admitted to coke use AND stealing his place in the joint rotation. But I get this damn look. Obama was out there, intercepting joints and I get this look.

"Oh shit… Monica… we need to pick up my car too."

■ ■ ■

I am not a man of God. I believe in something bigger and better than us, something god-like, but I can't understand why that being would want me in a big stone building for an hour every Sunday. I truly doubt God is such an egomaniac. Where's the profit in that?

It's not that I have anything against churchgoers. That's all well and good. It is the purpose of religion to calm the soul and nurture the spirit, and if church does that, so be it. I prefer hockey. No big dif.

Father Tim, on the other hand, is obviously quite a man of the cloth. He's the prototype of the Irish Catholic priest. A balding mane of red hair, a thin beard tight to his chubby face. His voice thunders and projects, thunders and projects. His greeting, "And good afternoon to you and may God bless", tweaked my hangover. His smile was electric, 2000 watts.

"So, are we ready to walk through the ceremony?" The church was well lit. The twenty-four chandeliers were going and there was plenty of sunshine pouring through the stained glass. "Well, God shall walk us through this, this ceremony of love and commitment." Indeed.

"Oh, what a beautiful chaste Christian couple." U-huh. Chaste. Right.

Make this go away.

"Monica, walk with your shoulders back. Allow your beautiful body to bask in God's beautiful love" Hey, that's my girlfriend, pal.

This is hell on Earth.

"Now, William, pay attention while you wait in front of the alter. Eyes down the aisle, but body ready to adore the Lord. Swivel at your hips."

This is turning into a music video. This isn't a sacrament anymore.

"Keep your bodies facing, but turn your faces just a little towards the audience. This is their show too."

Ok, this is hell. I can't believe what I'm hearing.

"And on your exit, walk at the same gait but a little quicker. You're happier now, you're married in the eyes of God."

Where is a stray bullet when you need one?

"Ok, let's run through this one more time, this time with *feeling*."

I can feel my soul tear. My blood begins to itch.

"William, are you paying any attention to a word I'm saying?" Damn, this is real.

"Sorry, a little distracted. I'll pay more attention, Father."

For another 40 minutes, Father Tim waltzed my fiancée and I around the church, a choreography worthy of an Oscar. Still, I prayed for release.

Any release.

■ ■ ■

Dinner was nice. We ate at some Jewish deli down the block from the church. Monica told me about the final confirmations, told me about the final this and the final that.

Right.

Men just don't seem to get all wrapped up in weddings like women. All those dozens of "Bride" magazines and websites, but practically no "Groom" anything. How many guys do you know give a flying fuck about what color the napkins will be at the reception, let alone what shape the pats of butter will be? Men as a gender do not care about who sits with whom, what high school the DJ went to, or whether the rice that may or may not be thrown will pose any danger to the birds that will inevitably eat it.

Apparently, these are things.

Don't get me wrong. I am very excited about the wedding and all the upcoming festivities and social upheaval. It's all rather invigorating and nice, but it's not The Occasion that it is with women. It's cool, let her get excited.

I was taking the night off from drinking, so after dinner, Monica and I Netflixed *The Big Lebowski*. I tried to talk her into streaming a porno but she wasn't down with that. She's so cool about sexual stuff all the time, but she can't stand porn. She doesn't even like me to watch it.

One time, maybe the second time we went away just us somewhere, skiing I think, I brought a movie along with me-yes, I used to own a few porn DVDs. A little something to spice the evening up with. Nothing hardcore, just standard one-on-one porn. I'm not talking *Anal Avengers in Luscious Lube Land* or *Cum Splattered Dildo Whores* or anything offensive. She flipped out, saying that maybe she just wasn't enough woman for me, that all these movies did was demean women and treat them like objects.

Civilized people, she told me, don't need porn, they have imaginations.

Whatever. What guy is going to give up porn?

After the movie, we went to bed. We desperately needed the rest. Monica's bachelorette party was tomorrow and mine was the day after. Tomorrow I was going out with the guys from work. I think I have an important meeting tomorrow around 2ish, kind of wish I did call work today. Details would be nice, but I'm sure someone covered for me. The walk of the privileged is, in and of itself, its own reward.

With a good night's sleep, I would be ready to tackle the next few days. These were the days right here. Everything was falling into place. Pieces of a puzzle settling into place.

5

Breakfast is toast, OJ, and the newspaper.

ESPN.

Facebook.

Email.

Then CNN or FoxNews if there's time.

Monica is already gone for work. I shower and shave and put on a power tie. Well, a nice argyle one, blue and red. I think Monica may have bought it for me (a birthday, maybe?) but my mom could have given it to me. These really aren't things I need to remember.

Driving to work, I listened to Weezer's *Pinkerton* and only swerved violently in front of other cars at high speeds two or three times. I don't suffer from road rage or anything, I just like to keep everyone on his or her toes.

It gets their hearts going with the quickness. For just a brief, simple second, they are happy to be alive.

They feel lucky. Honored.

Like God really actually loves them individually.

Like they are a special, meaningful cog in the eternal machine.

It makes them feel like they matter, after all. Like they have a guardian angel, if you will.

Think about it. You're driving to a nine-to-five that you hate and you'd quit but you need the medical coverage because the damn second you don't have any, your kid or wife gets pneumonia or breaks a leg or something. You have laundry to pick up and bills that need you need to *3 on your cell and you'd better be at the tee ball at six so your kid knows you love him and all of a sudden you realize that you may hit a car at 65 mph and collide head on with the concrete median.

Your complete life flashes in front of your eyes.

You flash to your family and friends, gathered around your casket on a rainy day with some priest droning on about God taking you too soon.

And you're still alive.

You're flipping me the bird and laying on your horn but guess what? I just redeemed your soul. They call this salvation.

Deliverance.

Rescue.

Liberation. Release. Some people pay $225 per hour for this, and you get it for free.

You're welcome.

And then you hate me. And I'm ok with that.

6

My secretary Megan greets me as I get close to my office. She was at the copier apparently.

"Mr. Meridan-"

"Bill. Just call me Bill."

"Bill. Um, you ok?" Monica called yesterday and you didn't and I tried to call you but there was no answer and I thought something was up."

"Oh, sorry about that. Hangover, massive hangover. Then we had Mass walkthrough with Father Richard Simmons Jr. What an ordeal."

She gives me that *if I nod my head you'll go away* look. She hands me my fan mail as I walk by and right before I get into my office, I look over my shoulder, and yeah, she's texting her boyfriend again.

I settle behind my desk and curse under my breath that I forgot a cup of coffee. Just as I am mentally weighing the repercussions of asking Megan to get me a cup the phone rings and Megan is on the intercom saying it's a fan.

So take a message. And can I have a cup of coffee?

"No way, Bill. She's called, we're talking, six or seven times today already. Total weirdo. You have got to get rid of her. Bill."

And the cup of coffee, I ask.

And all I can hear is her laughing and clicking away on her keyboard.

"William Meridan here."

"Oh my goodness, it's you. Really *you*. Say 'a weekend of sun and fun at the beach' for me. Please?"

Stupid marketing campaign, giving me a catchphrase. Fine. Fuck my life. I'll say it.

"Oh my goodness, that was incredible. Remarkable! Simply sensational!"

Um, yeah. Then you should see me when I actually fucking care.

"Well anywho, the reason I'm calling is to ask a minor wee little favor. My name is Sara Fisher and I'm getting married in a month, August 10, actually, and it's outdoors, so I need sunshine, and since you're getting married too, congrats by the way, I thought you'd understand."

Christ, one of these whack-jobs. Here it goes again.

"Well, I don't actually control the weather, but check the forecast the week prior for an accurate prediction. Thanks for calling. Bye." Click.

■ ■ ■

Like I don't have enough crap to do with the wedding coming up, today I'm at some science fair doing my obligatory live feed for the five o'clock show. I'm the special guest judge, and hey- I have the ribbon to prove it.

When I get there, the principal is all in my face, telling me the things I need to know about the contest.

There's two categories- earth science and theoretical science. The project is only going to be 75% of their score, the last quarter is going to be their presentation of their project. I'm supposed to not only look at their research, but the style and approach they use presenting it. Sure.

I'm telling you now, the volcano is going to win.

I'm walking around, looking at the projects like I care. Like they found the cure for cancer. Like with their hard work, Walt Disney can now be brought back to life.

Oh, look. A potato used as a battery. How original.

One of the teachers comes over to me and asks for my autograph. She opens her autograph book and flips through a few pages. "Wait, wait, I want you to sign next to Al Roker. You're both TV people, you know."

I nod my head like that's *the* most profound comment I've ever heard and scribble my name. I hand her back her book and keep going, checking out a model of the solar system and something on biodegradable trash bags but the teacher stays right next to me.

"You must be proud to be here. It's some accomplishment," she tells me. "We always get a big celebrity to do this, and this year, well, we just had to have you."

Yeah, I'm so proud of this that when I'm done, I'm rushing home to add it to my resume. I'm going to use this very experience to negotiate a better contract next time. LinkedIn, here I come.

It's getting close to five twenty-one, when I go live with the winner, so we hold our voting. The school makes a big deal about this, so we have to go to the girl's locker room and "vote behind closed doors". There was no volcano so I just vote for the same kid as the person who voted in front of me.

We got out into the gymnasium and at center court, there's the little icky shit with a blue ribbon on his shirt, standing in front of my camera. My camera guy is starting the thirty second count down. The kid's name is Brad.

Twenty-five seconds.

The cue cards are readied and my hair gets a final touch. Twenty seconds and counting.

All the preparation that goes into this, you'd expect a space shuttle to lift off.

Ten seconds to go and I'm reading the cue cards to myself, in my head.

We go live and I'm telling everyone where I'm at. I rattle off the 24 hour summary and introduce the winner. I ask him if he has anyone he wants to say hi to and the icky little shit says no, then sneezes into his hand, looks at a piece of snot that just maybe could be part of his frontal lobe, wipes it on my pants and gives the camera the bird.

■ ■ ■

I hung around the office, waiting for everyone else to wrap their business up for the day. I played a little Hearts on the computer and straightened my desk while I waited and waited and waited. Seconds drained by. Everything was slow and dragged out. A glitch in the time-space continuum. The Byzantine Empire existed for 1,123 years and 18 days, from March 11, 330 (it's founding by Constantine the Great) until May 29, 1453 (it's conquering by Ottoman Sultan, Mehmet II) and I was feeling every decade personally. Time grinds to a complete and utter halt. I'm not quite sure, I could be wrong and everything, but is it me or does this tropical depression look like Elvis?

By 4:15, most people were ready to go, the rest would catch up. Before leaving, I called Monica at her office. "Have fun tonight, babe. Don't get too wasted."

"Same goes for you, Bill. Be safe tonight."

"Every night, sweetheart, every night. Have a good time. Love you."

"Love you too."

We are at some dark stank bar, a few blocks from work. They have a good happy hour and shortly, the 7 or so of us made quick work of 5 pitchers. Things were slowly fuzzing up and it was quite a good thing. People from work were trickling in and by 6:00 we had half the bar and a third of the tables. People love an excuse to drink.

Like I'll never go out for beers when I'm married or something.

There apparently are these rules about bachelor party etiquette, especially involving alcohol. I was made aware of a custom, "dating back to the dawn of man", calling for me to drink a shot of tequila for every girl you had slept with prior to marriage. I managed to beg this one off until tomorrow night, claiming it was my official bachelor party. I was already way too drunk to handle tequila like a man. Or even as a little boy, for that matter.

I was talking to Paul "Ass Pirate to the Stars" Waters and Neil Zuelig. Both of them are bachelors. Paul has a couple of those on-again-off-again type girlfriends and I think Neil is a closet case. He worked in Accounting as an "empiricist". Right.

Paul turns to me and says, "So do you really think that you can go the rest of your life just sleeping with the same person? I mean, you have another fifty years or so of sex left and with Viagra, you could be playing 'hide the weenie' into your eighties. That's a long time. I mean, what's the longest you've ever been faithful?"

"Let's see… hmm… it would have to be Monica, so a little over three years now. The sex is good, I'm not worried about that in the least."

"But fifty years?"

"Christ, Paul. Why are you talking about this crap? Could you get a man a beer and shut the fuck up?" I had a smirk on my face so he'd think I was only playing around. It's fine if he thinks that, we do work together, but I loathe this vile, little, petty, man. He talks and talks and talks and talks about the most repetitive shit I could ever think up.

The person who taped the "Heave A Brick At Me" sign on his back last week, yeah, that was me.

And this guy says the most inappropriate stuff possible. He told Jim McPhae, who just lost a testicle to cancer, that since he'd have less semen hanging around, he wouldn't have to rub one out at work anymore, he could just wait until he got home.

The poor guy already felt emasculated, why not just toss some public humiliation on top.

It wasn't like everybody didn't know about Jim's at-work manual release therapy, but what of it? So? You'd be surprised, a lot of guys, and even a handful of women, take matters into their own hands at work. I've done it on occasion. Sometimes you need to take a little of the top before a big date or something.

Example: Your girlfriend has been out of town for over a week and she's coming straight from the airport to pick you up. You know as soon as you step through the door, the clothes are coming off. Now, you don't want this to be a quick thing here. You want full blown longevity and passion and three minutes won't cut it. You need to tap a teste in the afternoon to make sure a pleasurable experience is had by all.

It's about her. I swear.

Jim just made a regular thing out of it. It was a matter of fact, a law of nature that Jim would stroke off after lunch. It was clockwork; you could set your watch to it, usually.

Paul returned with the beers. Neil and I were discussing why people drink to intoxication despite all the pitfalls, hangovers, DUI, vomiting, the outrageous prices of beer and shots at bars and clubs. I thought it was a primitive impulse, a branch of man's hunter-gatherer instinct.

Neil thought it was simple self-destruction. You know it's bad for you. You know you're torturing your kidney and liver. You know it'll dehydrate you.

It's like saying your body may be a temple, but nothing lasts forever.

You don't want to leave a beautiful corpse. That's just wasteful. Everything that's ever been beautiful, Neil tells me, we try to destroy it.

Nice rainforest, let's cut it down and replace it with concrete. A fucking parking lot.

We need the ozone to protect us from ultra killer light waves, let's put holes in it.

This beer is killing me, barkeep, another round please.

Stake your claim he tells me. Mark your territory. Then trash it, because, man, that's your God-given right. Smoke that cigarette. Have unprotected sex. It's not like the Sistine Chapel is still looking that hot, if you get Neil's drift.

Build it up to tear it down. The day you're born, he says, you started dying. Why not add a personal touch to it? A little personality, some flair to your demise.

The kick in the teeth, he says, is you have to pace yourself a little in the process. There's no big, all-at-one time way to do. Suicide, he says, is a cop out. Anyone can pull a trigger or handle a knife or tie a noose or pop open a jar of sleeping pills. He tells me the real skill is riding the downfall for as long as possible.

I'm not thinking Life of the Party but I can't blame you if you were.

I was slurring my words a little and felt vaguely hungry so I suggested we move on to Slim's. Slim's had a great grill and two dollar drafts after 9. Being the guest of honor, my motion was quickly seconded and passed. I grabbed a cab with Neil and two girls. One was a secretary, Dan King's, I think, and the other worked in Human Resources. Neil may have been hitting on the HR girl, but if "So where's your parking spot?" is your idea of a pick-up line, you may well prove to be a stalker.

I feel so bad for repressed homosexuals sometimes. The attempts, if I can call them that, only serve to delay his inevitable coming out of the closet. As long as he's making an effort with the ladies, his mother smells grandkids for sure.

We arrive and Slim's was crowded but we quickly assimilated and dispersed. I managed to avoid Paul and chill with Neil at the back of the bar, near the jukebox and the bathroom. When you're in a bar, this is the best place to be. All the girls will have to walk by you numerous times and you can strike up an easy conversation with womenfolk at the jukebox. Not that I'm picking up women, mind you, I'm just letting you know for your own good.

Neil turned out to be pretty funny. He would point to two people at the bar, and then say what he felt they should really be saying. He called it White Trash Community Theatre and he was kind enough to narrate it for me.

"(in the narrator voice) Look here, as the male, made brave from imbibing the sacred elixir, walks up to the female and begins to initiate the breeding process. (in a deep male voice) Why, hello there, sexy lady. Fuck me if I'm wrong but you want to screw me. Oh *yeaaaaaaaah*. (in a petite female voice) Tee-hee. I wanna have your baby. Knock me up and leave me. (narrator) Now watch as the male proves his masculinity. (male) My dick is so big I'm already fucking you tomorrow. Oh *yeaaaaaaaah*. (female) Tee-hee. Slap me around, big daddy. Make me your lil bitch."

Neil chugged the rest of his beer and stumbled to the bathroom. Another perk of being so close, less chance you fall on your drunk face. I ordered some stuffed potato skins and a bowl of chili. I wasn't sleeping at Monica's tonight and I'd probably have the shits anyway. Neil didn't order anything, claiming to be on a strict liquid diet of beer and vodka.

When you are on a long bender, one of those real tears, you realize the most surreal things you could never begin to fathom sober. Things blur together. People's faces look the same, every song on the radio sounds the same, like one long continuous song. You feel inert, static, like you were in a vacuum. Your brain pings and buzzes out of boredom and you are never really alert to your surroundings. You are frozen, looking out with ice eyes, cold and blank and distant. Emotions seem stale, almost forced and you long for the inevitable release of sleep or death or unconsciousness or a coma or whatever. You feel entombed in your own body. Time loses all sense of proportion and dynamism, words always fall short of intended meaning. Everything looks like you have Vaseline smeared over your eyes. The only thing you can truly understand, the one thing engraved in your mind is: EMPTY.

Or maybe I'm just drunk.

A couple of hours later, I'm sufficiently bombed and sent home in a cab. My coworkers are even so nice as to pay for the cab ride for me. It's the little things people do to let you know they appreciate you. I managed to not throw up or pass out in the cab. I am home.

I stumble into the elevator and hit the 6 and crash on the comfy red felt couch while I wait for an elevator to descend. The elevator hiccupped on the sixth floor and I I almost lost it. Thankfully, it proved to be a temporary loss of sobriety. I maneuvered the hallway and closed in on my door. I fumbled with the key like a fifteen-year-old boy with breasts. I opened the door and entered.

I check my cell before passing out and I'M POPULAR! I have messages.

The first message was my mother, saying her and my father would be flying in tomorrow afternoon and maybe could we do lunch? Too bad, I just couldn't pencil them in.

The next message was from Monica, calling from the bachelorette party. She sounded loaded, worse than me. She said she was having a blast, that she POSITIVELY was not drunk and that she loved me with all her heart. She repeated this 15 or 20 times. It was sweet as hell.

The last message was from Brian Shapiro, my best man. He told me he'd be at my apartment by 4, that he was taking me out for dinner; "big, juicy steaks and a Cuban cigar" were promised. He wished me a good night and I promptly passed out in my bed, shoes still on.

7

Miraculously, the next day I arose. I showered, caught as much *Sportscenter* as I could and departed for the florist's. Monica had some retarded idea that I knew enough about the flowers to make sure that our flowers would be correct. To the best of my knowledge, I thought they were correct. As it would turn out later, they were wrong. No chrysanthemums. Damn me.

Spoiler alert- It's not like it would matter in the long run, just between you and me.

After that, I drove out to Monica's office. Monica worked for some foundation that did work for abandoned children, an orphanage type thing. If you were under 18, you could stay in a dorm type thing as long as you went to school. If you were over 18, they found you a decent job. It was a good foundation, set up by the grandson of the guy who invented the pet rock. It's a small world and getting smaller all of the time.

I bought some flowers from the florist's. She is in love with daffodils but they couldn't fit her little flower design scheme, so I had picked up a dozen. It's never too early into a marriage to score a few points. She put them in a vase and gave me a kiss.

"Rough night last night, Monica? The voicemail led me to believe you might not be in today."

"Oh. That message. Yeah. Long night." Nervous giggle.

"Nice try. You don't remember. That's fine. You sounded pretty 'faced. You kept saying how much you love me and how you weren't drunk at all."

"Have you heard about this thing about shots of tequila and-"

"Yes, and I don't want to know. I was hoping you were drunk on something else." How many fucking shots we talking here?

"Oh, I was, I was." She flashed me her big doleful eyes. God, she's hot.

Monica needed to get a lot of things done before we left on the honeymoon. We were going to Peru, to visit Inca ruins at Supe and Cajamarquilla. If we could work out a day trip, we would hit the Galapagos Islands.

I left and went to get a haircut. I went to the barbershop across from my old elementary school, now a vocational high school. My haircut was free, as was the tradition for all soon to be grooms at this particular shop. I know this because I've been getting my haircut here for twenty years.

I returned to my apartment a little after 3 o'clock. I head over to the fridge to grab a quick snack, and spot two bloated, floating orange masses at the top of my fish tank. Huh. I don't think i've feed them for a few weeks. Well, fuck me.

I turned on *The Big Lebowski* again and waited for Brian.

Brian showed up, late as usual. We watched the remaining 20 minutes of the movie and left for dinner. Brian owned a used bookstore down by the university. He loved his store. He got to spend all of his time around books *and* college girls. He took me to this old beat up looking steak house in a part of town I wasn't familiar with.

"This place has excellent steaks," he assured me, "plus, they don't care if we smoke these." He pulled two cigars and two joints out of his pocket.

"Alright then." We entered.

The place was dead. While we looked at the menu, we both lit our joint. The waiter came over, gave us each a glass of water, took our order (two king cut rib-eyes, medium rare, smothered in fried onions and mushrooms), and left.

"So, big night tonight, Billy." He smiled widely, nodding his head.

"Sure is. So how many people are showing up?"

"Counting strippers and hookers?"

"No, they don't count as participants. They are paid workers, man, hired help."

"Then almost 60. Big turn out because you're such a wonderful guy."

"Oh, don't make me blush. I'm flattered, dear boy." I've known Brian since high school. He's a really cool guy. He's always been there for me. Back in high school, Brian used to eat dinner over every night. We stopped even asking my mom and just set him a plate.

Our steaks arrived, big juicy hunks of cow flesh covered in onion and mushroom. A salad came as well, thick with

chickpeas and radishes. The salad and steak both looked deli-
cious and at first I didn't know which to start with, but the car-
nivore within won. The steak was perfection on a plate. It was
butter soft and melted in your mouth like, um, well, butter.

We finished our meals and lit those Cubans up. Brian assured me they were real Cubans. "They were smuggled over
with a Yankees pitching prospect," he claimed. One never
knows these days. Not being an expert on cigars, I can't truly
understand the greatness of a Cuban, but it was still pretty
fucking good.

We left and I called Monica one last time, to say good
night, I love you, that sort of crap. That taken care of, we em-
barked towards the hotel where the party was to be at.

It's a short ride over and we make every light. We valet
the car, stride into the lounge and enter a waiting elevator. We
bound out, almost strutting down the hall. Finally, we reach
the suite.

I entered the door and everyone cheered and hollered. It
felt quite nice and I laughed and smiled like a moron. There
were a freaking ton of people, Dennis and Mike and Rob and
Dave, Mike and Timmy from high school, 20 guys from work,
holy shit, Jimmy Elkins flew in from California, and at least 15
other people I haven't met or only seen once or twice.

We began drinking heavily.

There were two kegs and over twenty bottles of varying
fermentation. Some people were playing Quarters, other had a
rousing game of Asshole going. A joint and a few bowls were
making the rounds. A few guys were doing lines off a CD
jewel case and I went over for a bump. I was feeling like the

man. I was confused why a CD jewel case was present though. No one has a smallish mirror? Kinda bush league, guys.

People were coming up to me, almost one after another, congratulating me, wishing me condolences. Saying the same tired old jokes, keeping me from drinking. Finally, Brian saved me.

"Oh, Billy, look at what we have...pornography...on a DVD...on a 72-inch TV...Dolby Digital surround sound. Oh, Billy, I have three words for you.

Multiple.

Camera.

Angles."

He waved the DVD in front of my face. There were no pictures on it, no nothing, except one red sticker that read, "Adult Material. Minors Forbidden." on it. The disk itself said *Freaky Deaky Cum Guzzling Slutbags Vol 17 First Time on DVD!* How can a man pass this up? If you were gonna have cum guzzling slutbags, you need to have them freaky deaky style, and obviously this series is quality if it's on it's 16th sequel.

We popped it in and waited. At first there was this woman, giving some lecture about how pornography was to be used either as a martial aid or for masturbation and masturbation was perfectly normal and that none of the women in *Freaky Deaky Cum Guzzling Slutbags* were treated in a disrespectful manner. Instead, this movie promoted respect for women.

Indeed. I was raised to respect freaky deaky cum guzzling slutbags.

Finally, the movie started, a nice oral sex scene in a hot tub. Though it looked a little uncomfortable for the guy to be standing like that in the tub, I'm sure he's not complaining. People just kept entering the scene. After maybe ten minutes, there are 14 or 15 guys and 5 girls, a real orgy.

Then the world went away.

"Hey, that chick looks like Monica!"

Fade to black and good night.

8

"Yeah, that does look like Monica!"

"Oh shit! It is! That's Monica." By now, the whole world has totally gone away.

"Which one is Monica?"

"The one getting sodomized by the fat Italian guy."

"The one in the hot tub?"

"No, not that one. The one that's blowing that other dude, too." I am silent. I am invisible. I have never even been here before.

In the National Museum in Mexico City, there is a round stone alter with statues carved all around it, maybe seven or eight feet across. Over a million people had their heart cut out on it by the Aztecs. To celebrate the reign of a new king, thousand would perish.

"Wow, look at her tits. They're pretty perky, Bill." I am not looking at what is NOT going on in front of me.

"Damn, he blew his load already. Talk about a facial." I do not exist.

In the Battle of Marathon, Herodotus tells us over 6,000 Persians were killed in combat, but less than 200 Athenians ceased to live. A Pheidippides ran the 26 miles back to Athens to share the good news and promptly dropped dead. Hence, the ancient marathon marathon. The modern 26.2 mile marathon is just a lazy queen.

"Oh my God. Double penetration. This right here, this is fucking quality." I am a void. I am an abyss. Blackness.

I'm not thinking Where's The Beef but I can't blame you if you were.

"Does she let you go Greek at home? A girl like that is hard to find."

In 1799, Czar Paul I of Russia got upset while examining his guards and commanded them to march to Siberia, a 2,000-mile trek across the frozen Russian tundra. They did as ordered, and were never heard from again.

"I've never seen a dick in her pussy and one in her ass before."

I'm guessing Father Tim was *a lot* further off with that whole chaste thing than I previously considered.

"Check out those camera angles, I want a better view." Oblivion sets in, existence disappears.

"Man, that's a tight ass. And he is totally violating it!"

On August 24, 79 AD, Mount Vesuvius erupted and buried the city of Pompeii, killing all inhabitants. Stop me if you heard that one before.

"Holy fuck! Lesbian action! Damn, your girl can eat a beaver." The soul is not mortal, the soul is not mortal, the soul is not mortal. "She's fuckin' working that clit!"

"He's tea bagging her. Look at him teabag her."

Well, she would have had to have ten shots of tequila due to this movie alone.

The Old Testament book of Joshua tells that on the day that the great Israeli general Joshua took the city of Makkedah, he "put the city and its king to the sword and totally destroyed everyone in it. He left no survivors." This is the devastation God planned back then.

This is what he does now.

I am not here. I have never been here. I will never be here. Here is an impossibility now and forever. Prepare for emergency crash landing, thank you for flying Fuck You Air. Upon descent, you will plummet out of control, spinning endlessly and aimlessly until you crash and burn crash and burn crash and burn crash and burn. There is no exit. There is not here. Not any more. The world has gone away. Everything is gone now. I am not here anymore.

■ ■ ■

It was ten o'clock when I got home from my bachelor party.

Ten o'clock PM.

Not AM like it should have been.

I was alone. And sober. It amazing how how realizing your lips have played One Degree of Kevin Bacon with numerous porn cocks can ruin a nice coke buzz.

I immediately called Monica. After brushing my teeth with a bar of soap. Sand paper? Probably overkill.

"So, want to guess what I saw at my bachelor party?"

"Saw? It's already over? Did something happen Are you ok?" Not in any sense of the word, no, I'm not ok.

"Oh, come on. Just guess."

"William, I haven't the faintest. What, oh what ever did you see?"

"*Freaky Deaky Cum Guzzling Slutbags*. Volume seventeen, was it?" Silence but I could hear her eyes rolling over my cell. "Did you know that on some new DVD movies, you get multiple camera angles? No, really. You can. I got to see you, Monica, my fiancée, get sodomized by a woman with a strap on while performing oral sex on both a man and a woman, all in 360 degrees of motion. It was like I was in the room. It was like everyone else at the party was in the room. *They* found it funny. Do you think *I* found it funny?" Silence. "By you not talking, I will grant that you realize I would not find your starring role in a porno the least bit amusing."

"Calm down, William, I can explain."

"Explain? Explain? Explain the double penetration? Explain the homosexual activity? Explained why this was filmed last year? We were ENGAGED last year. Did you NOT realize that being in a pornographic movie would require you to have sexual relations with a person or persons who were not your fiancée?"

"Of course I knew that. Do you think I'm stupid?" Stupid isn't quite the word but I'm willing to settle. "William, my reasons for doing those movies had nothing to do with hurting you. And it's over now."

"Whoa, whoa, whoa. Movies? Plural- movie*SSSSS*?"

All I'm wondering here is did she have to do shots for the girls she's slept with too?

"Well, yes, plural. More than one." Thanks for the definition on that, us non-porn stars aren't quite with it.

"How many?"

"Does it matter?" Oh, on so many different levels does this matter.

"Yeah, it matters, believe me. How many?"

"Six. Plus cameos in two others."

"And how many while you were with me?"

"All of them." Think atomic shrinkage right here, we're talking I'm a freaking innie now. Straight to mangina territory.

"Ok, we need to talk, I'm coming over." I hung up and went down to my car.

My mind was all over the place. Random images popped up, went away, appeared again. My brain was like the screen of a virus infested laptop.

I can't think of an appropriate description of my mental state but a flashback on crack seems adequate.

A nightmare train going through a dark tunnel. Flashes of lightening. For some reason, clowns.

How am I supposed to deal with something like this? What in the world is going to make this all just go away?

9

Suffice it to say, Monica did not have an elusive magic token that could make the whole porno thing go away. She wasn't embarrassed by it at all; she didn't think it was cheating on me at all. There's no violation of monogamy, she tells me.

Don't think of it as another guy's cock in me, she says, think of it as the down payment on a car. I like leather interiors, she reminds me.

Don't think of it as a facial, think of it as a vacation somewhere. A four day, three night all inclusive somewhere tropical. Just for letting five men ejaculate on her.

It's not anal sex, it's a shopping spree. It's not a gangbang. It's my Christmas present. You might think she was going down on another chick, but no- she's just paying off her credit cards.

She doesn't want me to think of it as cheapening our relationship. She wants me to think of it as an expression of love and mutual respect. I swear to God, she's keeping a straight face while she says this to me.

Or think of it as freeing her own sexuality.

"What, you can't free it with me?"

"Oh, William, you're just too, well, not *that* free."

We cancelled the wedding the next day due to "personal issues" that we did not disclose. We made it clear the wedding was cancelled, not delayed. There was going to be no rescheduling, hope you kept your receipts. Work gave me my honeymoon as sick pay.

Good thing too, because I was sick as hell. I wouldn't get out of bed, I wouldn't answer the phone. Life was depression, a wet wool blanket pulled over me. I didn't shower much and I ate only at the most random intervals. I didn't think at all. There was no purpose to thought because there was no purpose to life because there was no purpose of being.

Everything had been devalued now. China deals in currency devaluation? I deal in self devaluation now.

I was never sure if it was day or night- my shades were pulled tight as a drum and gave up on archaic concepts like "day" and "night" . Sure, there were still a few clocks in my apartment, but they were like pet hermit crabs. There, and supposed to have some value, but really, you just ignored them.

I would walk around my two bedroom apartment and just wander from room to room. I would find something to distract me for a few minutes, then I would put it down and walk away. I would pick up a book that was sitting there, open up to the middle and read a chapter or two, go into my bathroom and clean the basin out, go into the extra bedroom and nap for a few hours then go and alphabetize my DVDs. I would take hours fine tuning the naming convention of mp3s from concerts I'd downloaded.

...Lather rinse repeat lather rinse repeat lather rinse repeat...

I would turn on the stove to cook something, only to wander back an hour later to charred remains, smoldering, smoke filling the space. I slept on every surface in my apartment. Bathroom floor, kitchen floor, on the table, sofa, loveseat, hallway, hell, I even slept on the sofa table and my desk.

Life was suddenly an abstract painting. Some color thrown around, subtle tones to convey emotion, a blank meandering. Throw it in a blender and call it my life.

Everything but a meaning or purpose.

I read somewhere that scientists were afraid that some species of white panther were no longer mating. The last pair was in captivity but there were no baby almost-extinct white panthers and they exhibited no sexual arousal. The scientists tried everything, lowering the temperature, raising it, more moisture, less moisture, different food, different water, other toys, everything they could think of. They even tried playing jazz records with the light dimmed.

But the panthers wouldn't mate and those panthers nailed it on the head.

There's no point. So they have a cub. Who's the cub going to mate with? His sister? His mom? Yeah, that'll save the species right there.

I'm not thinking The Deep South but I can't blame you if you were.

I would order a pay-per-view movie and then not watch it. I would get bored half way through shaving and just leave the bathroom. Why bother? It would be there when I came back. Or not. So? It's not like it would save the non-fucking white panthers.

There were people trying to get me out of funk though. Brian called two or three times a day but I wouldn't answer the phone. My brother and mother tried a lot as well but to no avail. I sent them a brief text saying basically, I'm fine, leave me alone, thanks a million.

Jesus Christ could have called and offered me the Holy Spirit's job and an excellent health plan and robust pension and I wouldn't have picked up that phone.

■ ■ ■

There comes a time in every man's life where he is forced to reassess his worldview, to step back and reevaluate his current condition. There comes a time in a man's life where he must put aside prior ideas and conceptions, abandon the simple pursuits of childhood and move boldly into the bright light of manhood.

There come a time in every man's life when he is masturbating entirely too much.

It seems to me that my testes were accustomed to making enough semen for Monica and my sex life, which was at least once a day, you know, like ten times a week. That was fine. I could toss that off without breaking a sweat.

But it did nothing to make up for the physical closeness. There was no way to make up for it. And the whole problem is, guys don't think of it as Cuddling, we think of it as the Post-Orgasm. The aftermath of Mount Saint Helens blowing her top as the tiny flakes of ash and soot flitter down like dirty snow and cover the world in soul-fucking gray.

The volcano always wins.

It's also like the cast party after a play.

So I'd come. And I wouldn't be satisfied. So I'd jerk off again.

And not be satisfied.

Try to feel better.

And not in the faintest satisfied.

It's just like premature ejaculation. Women feel all cheated because we got off and they didn't. Trust me ladies, a premature ejaculation does NOT feel good at all. You are all NONO NOPLEASEDON'TNOTNOWBASEBALLSTATISCTICS DEADBODIESNONONO. Believe me with this one.

I was masturbating seven or eight times a day, easy. I would turn on my Playstation to play a game of hockey and in the middle of the first period, I would have a raging hard on you could chisel granite with. It would knock the controller out of my hand and start looking for a puck. Any puck.

I'm not thinking High Sticking but I can't blame you if you were.

Another big problem is there are only so many ways to spank it before it gets boring.

First you use hand lotion, then you go dry hump. With a condom on. Turn your hand upside down and go slowly and it feels like a slow blowjob. Rub against your mattress. A nice little finale to try to rub the big thick vein between your balls, the one that runs up the underside of your crank, as you're shooting. It's a nice little goodnight present.

Sometimes I would orgasm twelve times. It was getting ridiculous. My hand would cramp up, my wrist would collapse, my fingers would twitch and jerk and my forearm would seize up so I'd dry hump my pillow.

I haven't been this bad since I figured out how to jerk off in the sixth grade.

10

I was supposed to be married for a week today. The wedding would have been a week ago. We were supposed to start packing to come back from our honeymoon. But it wasn't because my then-fiancée failed to inform me of her budding porn career. I can not think of one piece of relevant personal information I didn't share with her. It's fine, though, because she would have been a terrible mother.

The things I say to make myself feel better...

I decided that today I should be around people so I call Brian at work.

"Hey."

"Bill? Oh, hey. What's up? Something wrong? You ok?"

"Yeah, I'm fine. Just calling to see what's up with what's going down. See if maybe you wanted to get together tonight, have a few beers or something."

"Yeah, sure. Give me an hour or so after I get off. Around seven, probably."

"Cool." I took a nap.

I never really fell asleep, but I was vaguely refreshed. For some reason, lying in bed listening to an old mix tape I made in high school, curled in the fetal position under three blankets with the room pitch black relaxed and comforted me. It was the return to the womb, a wonderful regression. Floating in embryonic bliss is the true wish of all late 20's/early 30's guys who don't have children. It's not true love or a better job or more money or a huge inheritance or a great stock portfolios- it is none of that. We want only nothing.

A perfect delicate nothing. No existence is better than a perfect existence.

Who says we don't set goals for ourselves?

Brian showed up at 6:20 so we watched the last ten minutes of *The Simpsons*. There is the perfect TV show. It's a truly American family.

But on Earth was I watching live television? Was I that far gone?

Anyway, Brian didn't say anything to me. I guess he was afraid to say the wrong thing, that I may flip out and dismember him. I was not in the mood for bloodshed, though.

"Well, how are you holding up?" Brian almost winced as he asked.

"About as well as you could expect, I guess."

"So, are you going to see Monica again?"

Besides in nightmares?

"No, no I don't think so. We made a clean cut. It's over. It's for the best though."

All lies. I didn't even believe it as I was saying it. Monica left a cut that ran deep and didn't heal. Like a nick on the roof of your mouth, that would heal but you can't leave it alone because it's right the fuck there. But it was true that I wouldn't be seeing her again.

"Yeah, there's nothing worse than sloppy seconds. Or fiftieths."

"Because I like you, because you are my friend, I'll bottle up my bile-filled visceral reaction and not kill you where you stand. I'm a nice guy."

"Of course you are. So, you going to stay in your apartment for the next few years or what?"

This is the exact same question I've been asking myself.

■ ■ ■

Why was I the walking dead? What was really bothering me? Was it that Monica had made a few adult movies where she had three penises in her at once? Or was it the utter collapse of my marriage-to-be? Could I simply be embarrassed? What did people think of me now?

First thing I needed to do was stop talking to myself.

Second thing I needed to do is focus on the positive. It's better I found out now, then after two feral kids and an enormous mortgage. Now I can find the right person for me. I will sell my soul for comfort.

I hate fucking feral kids.

Just keep lying to yourself. Maintain the myth. Shut up, me.

Third thing I need to do is take a shower. Hot water can work wonders, on body, mind, and on soul.

Fourth thing I need to do is to go back to work. I need a schedule again. Something to take the mind off things. I would sell my soul, but not my dick, for some comfort.

Just keep on lying.

I often wonder if we work to pay the bills or to distract us from the bills.

Fifth thing I need is a drink. Or is the drink a fifth. Either way, I'm in.

I call work and let them know I'll be in tomorrow. They tell me it's Friday. I've already had my shows covered for the week.

Hey. Why not just take the weekend off and just come in Monday?

Assholes.

■ ■ ■

Saturday my parents came over under the guise of getting back some luggage they had lent me when Monica and I went up-state for a weekend a few months back. Right.

My mother immediately grabbed my shoulder blades and gave me a hard wet kiss, leaving her mauve lipstick spread all over my mouth area. "How are you, honey? Feeling better?"

"Yeah, Mom. Cool as cool can be. I'm going back to work on Monday."

"Oh, that's wonderful, dear. We were so worried when you didn't call us back all week. You really shouldn't scare us like that. Did we ever scare you like that, William, did we? Nathan, did we ever scare him like that when he was a child?"

"No, dear, we did nothing of the sort," he muttered stuffing his hands in his pockets, looking sideways down my hallway.

Dad's not what you would call Man of the House or anything.

"No, William, we never scared you like that. Now, you on the other hand, were scared all of the time. You remember? You were 12 years old when you finally stopped running into our room at two in the morning once a week crying about the boogieman?" It was Freddie Krueger. You know, the dude was burned alive for molesting children and had knives for fingers, and oh fucking yeah, only killed you when you fell asleep. But sure. Scared of my shadow. What a pussy.

"I never said you did, Mom. You guys want something to drink? Please, come in."

This is going to break all known laws of nature and physics by sucking and blowing simultaneously.

My mother wandered off into my tiny kitchen. I gathered myself for the inevitable health food assault but my father drew first blood.

My dad is standing by the bookcase in front of one of those small tour date posters things that haven't been used since the 60's but still sell for $20 at flea markets. Anyway, it's Pearl Jam for a show they did in Boston my junior year.

"You still listening to that rock-the-roll crap? That garbage sounds like someone trying to make some loving to a cat. Screeching and banging and crashing. Now, Gershwin, that was great music. A gentle piano ballad with a tender melody."

Ugh. So lame. His heaven = my hell.

"William, why is there so much alcohol in your fridge? There's a twelve pack of beer, a bottle of vodka, two bottles of Goldshlager, a bottle of wine- TWO bottles of wine. Where's the soymilk...?"

I'm tuned out to the normal world salad.

Green.

Organic.

Hydroponic.

Non-insecticide.

Cod liver oil.

Twice a day vitamins.

"What's this? William, what's this?"

Cyanide, Mom, take it. Now.

"Um, that's bean dip I made a few days ago. Try it. Use the tortilla chips." She opens the bag, dips the chip and spits it out into the sink. Did I say a few days ago? I meant a few *weeks* ago.

Oops.

"That's horrid, William!" She storms off to the bathroom spitting. My father is still looking through my CD collection, which hasn't been maintained, added to, or even paid attention to since 2006 or so.

"Who is Pink Floyd? Is he gay? Who calls themselves Pink? No parent would call their son Pink. He must be gay."

"No, Dad, Pink Floyd is a band. It's a bunch of straight guys. They are all married, most of them more than once."

"Just because you're married doesn't mean a thing anymore. Everyone is a bisexual these days."

Right, pop. Transsexual. Bisexual. Trisexual. Omni-animal-sexual. It's like fucking a T Rex from behind and giving it a reach around just because it can't do it itself.

"William, your toothpaste is just terrible. It didn't do a thing for my teeth. It just slid around on my teeth and now my whole mouth feels sticky."

"What toothpaste did you use?"

"The one in your medicine cabinet. What was it called? K-Y Jelly, I think."

Indeed. Now I wonder if Monica used that as toothpaste too.

■ ■ ■

Sunday is a day of rest. More importantly, it is a day of NFL football. Of course, this being the middle of summer, I'm totally screwed on that one. Most importantly, it is my last day to prepare myself for my return to work. I am not quite sure I'm up to the social interaction needed to function in a workplace environment.

People will point and whisper. As I move through them, they part like the Red Sea.

Speaking of, recent scholarship indicates that Red Sea, as it appears in the Bible, may be a misinterpretation. They may have meant Reed Sea, a marshy inlet to the north of the Red Sea. This "sea" would flood for half of the year and be a dry swamp the other half. These scholars say that what might have happened is the fugitive Jews got through the Reed Sea and before the Egyptians came through, the area flooded, as it did seasonally. The sudden mud would have rendered it impassable to the chariots and horses the Egyptians relied on. Saying they died horribly is just typical Biblical overstatement. You know, like saying God loves me.

Like Lot's wife was really turned into a pillar of salt or some shit.

Still, I didn't want to feel like a leper. I know I could count on Paul to say something dumb. Hell, he'd probably say it two or three times before someone told him to shut up. Not to mention I have no real desire to work and now you see what I'm saying. It was supposed to be warm and clear for the next few days. How am I supposed to deliver good news at a time like this?

Still, I saw it there, looming like the next ice age. Fate is a glacier. You never see it in action, but over the course of your life, it moves you from point A to point B. And somehow, I had broke free on my own private ice floe. I felt like an old sickly Eskimo who realized he no longer served a purpose or had a goal higher than self-preservation. I was floating away into the next ice age.

I'm not thinking Catastrophic Global Climate Change but I couldn't blame you if you were.

Not that I'm complaining or anything. There is a restraining joy to be found when one attains total isolation in a crowded room. I was floating away to melt in the gulf stream with almost zero chance of sinking a ship. With all the fluorescent lights at work, if you squint really hard, people just disappear. Totally gone. Discreetly leave a paper in the copier that says "You have been chosen. Await further instructions. You know who this is. End." The Hundred Years' War lasted longer than one hundred years and could easily be divided into three or four distinct wars. There is peace in alone.

Hopefully, a good night's sleep is all I need. Right before bed I drank a warm cup of cocoa and pulled a few tubes on my trusty bong. Now I lay me down to sleep.

I pray the Lord my sanity to keep.

For if I should die before I wake.

I pray the Lord my soul to break. Amen.

11

It was not until I arrived at work that I realized I hadn't spoken a word out loud in over two days. We're talking monk quiet here. Somehow, under the protection of God maybe, I made it to my office without a word. I closed the door behind me and collapsed on my desk. There were a few letters to open, a few reports to peruse.

Megan came in slowly, afraid to startle the caged animal. "Bill. Um. Bill, want a coffee?"

I said yes and she said ok and turned to leave. She came back with a hot cup of coffee and reminded me of a production meeting at ten o'clock. I thanked her and she left. I was alone again with a minimum amount of pain and discomfort.

The coffee was good and gave me that little jolt I needed to face a meeting today. That nervous edge to actually be productive.

I reviewed weather patterns in Western Canada. I looked forward to death. I sharpened a pencil. I inhaled oxygen. I left for the meeting.

Just in case anyone really cares, I should have been to Peru by now.

I walked into the room, casual, suave, nonplussed. I glanced around nonchalantly. I straightened my papers by clacking them on the table. Clack Clack Clack. I was in control.

"So, wow, like, what was it like? Sleeping with a porn star, wow! That's like every guy's dream and you did it. What was it like?" Oh, I see Paul has joined us today.

Lovely.

I rose slowly, turned gently. I laughed just a tad and looked around at all of the wide eyes. I squared myself to Paul and laughed a bit more. I reached over and straighten his tie and laughed loudly. I took a step closer, put my right hand on his shoulder and whispered in his ear.

"Listen, Paul, buddy. I want you to take this as *constructive* criticism, not *destructive* criticism. It's real important to me that you understand that. Ok then. Now, all I want to tell you is if you ever EVER EVER say anything to me again that is not pertaining to work- one word that is either superfluous or personal- I will take you into the bathroom and fuck you up the ass while flushing your fucking head in the toilet. This is not a threat. Oh no, sir. This is most definitely a promise. Cross my heart and hope to die. Ok? I swear to God, I will tear a hole in your throat and fuck your esophagus. Another promise- you will swallow it too. Every bloody drop. Are we on the same level here, Paul? You know what, I'll make this easier. The only words you are ever to say to me are 'And now for the weather, Bill Meridian.' Get it?"

We sat down and the meeting began like nothing ever happened. Because nothing happened.

■ ■ ■

I went to lunch with Neil after the meeting. He had left a message with Megan to call him if I wanted to join him for Ethiopian down by the Art Museum. I wanted to leave the office desperately and Ethiopian cuisine sounded like just the oxymoron to provide sanctuary.

It was a dive of a restaurant. It looked like some poor person's dining room, with seven or eight tables. It didn't look African. It just looked inner-city American. We ordered a meat sampler and a vegetable sampler and a couple of beers. Neil looked at me pensively. He looked around vaguely and seemed as if he wanted to ask something.

"Just say it. Say you're sorry, it's all for the best. Go ahead, I'm cool about it now."

"Well, that's good but you look like shit. You been drinking?"

"No, but thanks."

"Well maybe you should. And I heard what you said to Waters. 'Fuck his throat'. Nice touch. He's going to crap himself every time he sees you now." Well, it's better than me crapping down his throat, I suppose.

We have a few more beers and the food arrives. In Ethiopia, there are no utensils. Instead, you pick up the food with bits of this gamy tortilla looking thing. The food, which looks like it may or may not have been digested already, has a nice simple flavor. Really nice, actually.

"If I can ask one question, how often do you think about Monica?"

Every second of every minute of every hour of every day.

"Not that much. I try to, you know, block it out. I really only think about her when I'm alone."

Every second of every minute of every hour of every day.

"That's totally understandable. If you ever need to talk or anything, grab a beer or twelve or something, just give me a call." He handed me his card. "I put my cell number on the back. Feel free."

"Thanks, man. Thanks a lot."

We finished our meals in relative silence. We had ten or eleven beers between us so we were feeling nice and lubricated.

We drove back to work in oppressive silence. Neil's one of those guys who takes driving very seriously. He honestly looked distracted by having the radio on. He kept two hands on the wheel at all times, at ten o'clock and two o'clock. He turned hand over hand. He came to a complete stop at stop signs. He always used a turn signal. He obeyed posted speed limits. He passed on the left.

He used his mirrors. He checked his blind spot. He looked both ways when he turned. He checked and rechecked just about everything. Maybe this was the five beers but he's taking this super serious.

Megan came up to me as soon as I was in sight. "Bill. Bill. Mr. Adkins wants to see you right away."

Chet Adkins is my immediate supervisor, the guy responsible for the noon and five o'clock telecasts. He never wanted to see me. I didn't think he even knew my name.

I took the elevator up to Chet's floor. I prayed for a fire. You aren't supposed to use elevators during a fire, you know. They call it a safety hazard. Like safety is always the hazard.

I walked into his office and told his secretary I was here. Without looking she pointed at a chair and I sat. This reminded me of how Monica used to dismissively point at things she wanted me to take care of without saying anything or, you know, looking at. Point to the trash can. The dirty shower. My boxers on the bedroom floor. And though this is getting me ten flavors of pissed off, I'm still starting to a chub thinking about her.

I'm not thinking Pavlovian Response but I can't blame you if you were.

A few minutes later, Chet's door opens and he says, "Bill. Come in." I entered and sat in a leather chair across from his desk.

"Bill, first of all, let me give you my condolences over your cancelled wedding. You have my sympathies and I know this has all been difficult for you, but that doesn't excuse threatening co-workers."

I said it wasn't a threat though.

"Bill, maybe you shouldn't have come back to work so quickly. Maybe what you need is more time to gather your thoughts. What do you think?" I think I can imagine Paul standing in a pool of his own tears, whimpering about mean old Mr. Bill. Thanks Paul, you douche canoe, once your check clears you'll be the proud new owner of knowing how a real man's balls feel against your dimpled chin when he's pissing up your nose.

"Bill, maybe you shouldn't have come back to work so quickly. Maybe what you need is more time to gather your thought and parse your feelings. What do you think"?

"But I told Paul I wasn't threatening him. I guess I may have overreacted just a little, but it won't happen again, I swear."

He just stares at me like there's more I'm supposed to say so I go, "I promise?"

"Bill, this isn't going to happen again. I want you to see this doctor." He handed me a business card. I'm just racking up the cards today, boy. "I made you an appointment for to-morrow, ten thirty. If you feel up to it, you can come to work afterwards. Now go home and rest."

I nodded in numb agreement.

I went home. I went to sleep.

12

So now I'm supposed to be crazy. I'm supposed to have thoughts that are wrong. I am supposed to stalk the president and save my urine in jars.

I'm supposed to hear voices that propose violent activities and I'm supposed to agree. I'm supposed to think aliens are behind it. I'm supposed to have hallucinations.

Yeah, now I'm going to be seeing shit; spiders and shadows and shit.

I'm supposed to be fucking crazy.

I have so got to stop talking to myself.

Lots of people, normal people, go to therapists. Every one has problems. Every single living human being has issues.

We all had crappy childhoods. We were all abused. We are a world of addicts. Totally diseased.

I mean, even the Dali Lama has nightmares.

Whether it's alcoholism or depression, you're messed up somehow. Mild paranoia or bipolar disorder, it's your trip.

It's like half the world is in therapy now, but you have to wonder if the other half needs it more. Can you be too screwed up if you realize you're screwed up?

I'm not thinking Catch-22 but I can't blame you if you were.

I think I did what anyone who finds out 37 hours prior to marriage that your soon-to-be spouse is a porn star.

Her first movie was *Jurassic Pork*. Everyone dressed up as cave people (for a little bit) and they did it in caves. They used raw flame for lighting. Talk about ambiance.

You're God damn right I'm going to get violent over this.

No I'm not. I am going to remain calm. Breathe in, breathe out. Repeat. Happy place, happy place. Find my Zen place. Take a deep breath. Hold it. Let it out slowly. Calm, calmer, calmest.

My ex-fiancée was named "The Hardest Working Choad Freak in the Industry 2016." I have no clue what it means but it still pisses me off. Someone *needs* to die for this.

See? This isn't going to work. Maybe I do need to talk to a shrink, talk about this stuff. They say that just speaking the problem out loud is half the cure. Of course, the other half involves heavy medication. May or may not be fun.

But I'm not crazy. I'm not crazy. I may be entertaining the faintest notion of temporary madness, but I'm not crazy. I'm not insane or loony or neurotic or disturbed. I'm so not obsessed or hung-up or fixated or any of that. I'm no psycho.

■ ■ ■

I woke up early the next morning, feeling tired and run down. I always feel this way after I get a lot of sleep. It's like my body gets used to the sleep and can't kick it into gear when I finally wake up. I showered and ate and watched *Sportscenter.* After that, I left for the therapist's. I knew where it was because it was in the same building as my father's lawyer. I spent an afternoon there when my father changed his will.

I sat in the waiting room for five or ten minutes. Eventually, the receptionist came over with some paper work for first time patients.

Any history of diabetes in the family?

Multiple Personalities Disorder? Syphilis?

Liver problems?

Arthritis? Any allergies? Recent surgeries?

Blackouts?

Do you own any guns?

Am I on any medication? Ever suffer from bouts of dizziness?

And are there any heart complications? History of hernias?

Next of kin? Primary care physician?

After this brief recap of my medical history, the therapist sees me. He greeted me in a most serene manner. He invited me to sit in a big comfy leather chair. He asked if I was comfortable, if I wanted anything to drink.

I shot a quick glance at my hands to make sure they aren't shaking. Nope. Ok. "No, I'm just dandy, thanks."

He asked me what happened with my fiancée and how I feel about it.

I stare at him. I stare through him.

What I feel is abandonment and isolation. What I feel is betrayed. What I feel is used. What I feel is violated, savaged, and twisted. What I feel is oblivion.

I told him how I found out about Monica's side job. He told me I had every right to be angry and embarrassed. I never said I was embarrassed, I tell him.

"Of course you didn't," he assures me, "of course you said no such thing."

I hate being patronized.

"But if you did feel embarrassed, it would be perfectly normal and natural to feel that way." Hooray.

He tells me it is understandable to have feelings of resentment and betrayal. He tells me that the only thing which undermines a man's confidence more than infidelity was impotence. Did I feel like my masculinity was being threatened?

Is this getting Freudian? Is my car a symbol for my penis? Do I drive my dick? Is he saying I could knock up a car wash? Is cutting people off akin to sword fighting?

There are no threats to my manhood, I tell him. No terrorist activity in my pants, thank you.

Wait. I could have AIDS. And not the Magic Johnson-you-can-live-forever-AIDS. I'd have the full blownsie AIDS. Thanks, Monica!

I ask if I can have a cup of coffee, lots of cream, please? He nods gently and gets up to get the drink.

I bet everyone asks for a cup of coffee here.

I am in over my head. This guy is good. He is *so* good. I think I might just make some shit up, just to have something to say.

He returned with the coffee. There was plenty of cream. He watched as I sipped from the cup. I told him it was good and he just nods and smiles like a senile old man. He asks if I am comfortable enough to discuss Monica with him.

What do you mean?

"Well, if something of that nature happened to me, I sure would have plenty to talk about." He looks at me. I stare back. "Maybe I can help you to sort out your feelings."

I feel like stone. Lead. I am shale, I am brick.

"What ran through your mind when you first saw Monica on the screen?" A bullet.

"Nothing, really. I just sort of went completely numb. I blacked out. I don't even remember going home."

"Ok. And...?"

"And nothing." Rocks don't bleed, asshole. Back off. "I guess I haven't really thought much about how I felt." What am I saying? Who have I become?

"Everything from then on is a cloud. A big fuzz. Really, I can't remember it. It's weird, you'd think it would be burned into my brain. But it's not. Why?"

He tells me it's a defense mechanism. Your mind represses what you don't want to hear. The things you just can't deal with. Think of it as benevolent Alzheimer's.

Instead of forgetting your children's names and faces, you forget about the time you walked in on your wife being railed by the mailman.

He asks if this may be the case.

"Well, I suppose it could be it. It's just been so much, blah blah blah words words words."

I continued to whine and cry like a baby. I moan on and on and he listens. He nods when appropriate. He looks concerned. He gets me Kleenex when needed. He clenched his lips tight like he actually gives a flying fuck.

He is God, in a godless world.

He wants to see me tomorrow. Yes, he wants to see *me* tomorrow. And I'll be here.

I'll be right here.

13

The next day I'm back at work a new man. Paul doesn't annoy me anymore. Paul is just another personal challenge. Not penetrating Paul's body is a moral victory. I am the better man for not having my penis inside him, and even better for not creating a new orifice to penetrate. Who knows at this point? Maybe that makes me *more* of a man.

I read my reports. I do research. I take Megan to lunch, you know, because I'm a new and improved kind of guy. Her pseudo-fag got a new job apparently. He's now a *customer service representative* for a furniture store out in the suburbs. But he's not gay.

I dictate a memo about how to save money thanks to some new website I read about on *Wired*. I attend a meeting on how time zones will save us money.

Sun light is money nowadays.

In only four hours I can see my therapist. I should apologize to Paul first.

Apologizing to him is the equivalent of the token they give people at AA meetings. It's proof you're better. Something you can squeeze in the palm of your hand.

He's not in his office when I stop by. I ask his secretary when he's due back but she doesn't answer me. It's not like I'm going to hurt the guy. I want a truce, smoke the peace pipe, bury the hatchet in a non-bloody fashion. I am a man of peace, not a man of violence. I hear a muffled sneeze from Paul's office.

I open the door and there's Paul, practically cowering behind his desk. For a sportscaster, there sure are a lot of pastels in this office.

"Paul, why are you hiding? I just wanted to apologize for yesterday. There's just a lot on my mind these days and I guess I vented all over you. Sorry." No eye contact. "You know I've been under a lot of stress. I didn't mean any of what I said." He still won't look at me. I guess I did lay it on sort of thick yesterday.

"Um, sure, Bill. No big deal. I understand. I should be more careful with what I say." No shit, Sherlock. "It's cool. I understand."

I am Gandhi. I am the Nobel Peace prize. I am the ambassador of goodwill among mankind. I am goodness personified.

I went down to the cafeteria and grabbed a snack with a few guys from Advertising. I tried hard to avoid people who had been at my bachelor party. I didn't need another Paul scenario, even if I was the warm fuzzy Zen center of all which is good.

I ate a salami sandwich. Everyone is talking about a movie I haven't seen. I drink an orange soda, no ice.

The movie is about some cowboys who get lost in a dust storm and resort to cannibalism to survive. You know, the Donner party with chaps and ten gallon hats. I went back to my office.

I sat behind my desk and waited. My appointment was at 5:15. It was only 3:45. To be on time, I should leave at 4:45. There might be traffic, maybe I should leave earlier.

Maybe I'm going overboard.

I ask Megan if she's gotten the weather forecast from the Pacific Rim yet. I ask if she's gotten directions to the dumb school where I get to judge between another volcano and a potato battery. I ask if my parents have called.

Her eyes widen and that pulsing vein on her right temple makes me think that her head might explode.

She recovers and tells me the Pac Rim readings will be arriving in ten minutes and she'll bring them right in. She's printed up the directions to the school and no, no one's called for me. But, she tells me, I need to have a written proposal for my new weekly live broadcasts.

Oh yeah, she adds as I'm walking away, that lady, the strange one, she called twice again today.

Her again.

■ ■ ■

I am safely in suite B-11 of the Farmington Hills Professional Building. I tell my therapist about my apology to Paul.

"Were you sincere? Did you mean what you said?" Huh?

"Not really. But that's what you wanted, for me to apologize. Right?"

It's not about what he wants, he tells me. It's about what I want. What I need. I need to do what's good for William he tells me.

Ok, this is getting too complicated.

My therapist wants me to communicate my feelings. He says I have emotions that I may not even realize. I could be into Broadway musicals for all I know. I'm not.

Art? Not me.

Classical music? Pass. Opera? Oh, I don't think so.

Poetry? Only if you count dirty limericks about a certain sportscaster on the bathroom stall wall.

He says I need to find these repressed feelings, they are the real me. I'm really on the inside, looking out he tells me. The defense mechanisms are covering up who William Meridan really is.

He thinks maybe I subconsciously knew about Monica being a choad freak. He thinks I knew she was getting sodomized on camera four or five times a year. He thinks I hid this knowledge because I hide a lot of things.

Did my father beat me?

Did my mother molest me?

Have I ever orally pleasured my brother?

Any babysitters who took advantage of me?

No. No. No. No.

Seriously, no one ever believes you when you say you had a normal childhood. It's just not possible. Nope, if you say it was fine, you're repressed. From a happy child to a repressed basket case in just two visits.

I think my therapist is the repressed one. But he listens so well.

I'll be back next week.

■ ■ ■

It's a Wednesday at six thirty so for sure I'm at my therapist's. Or it's Saturday at noon. Either way, here I am.

Today's task at hand is to regress past my childhood memories. Past the first things I remember. To infancy. Me in diapers, puking on everyone's shoulders.

What I'm in is a trance. A hypnotic state. An abstraction of sleep, if you will. This is what he tells me any way.

It's not like I'm faking it. I'm just in a good place where I'm trying to be agreeable. You know, go with the flow. Pleasant. Provide answers to satisfy the need, not necessarily the question. I'm pretty sure I'm not uncovering secret memories stored by my infant brain or unformed conscious. And it's not as much made up as it is the first thing off the top of my head. And hey, it's not like it's all my fault or anything.

That little white noise machine he has, the one that plays a crashing surf and crickets and a babbling brook, well, the brook just reminds me that my bladder is full. And it's hard to concentrate when you have to take a leak.

What I'm trying to say is I was trying so hard not to wet my pants I couldn't really put too much into this whole regression thing anyway.

Just keep lying to yourself.

And my therapist just keeps asking me these questions.

What do you see?

A room. My parents. Our dog. And I really have to pee.

What's the dog's name?

At first I want to say Lassie but that makes it obvious I'm phoning it in so today the childhood dog I never had is named Brandon.

What am I playing with?

A play phone. And my freaking teeth are floating in the Yellow Sea.

Just to make it interesting, today Mommy and Daddy are fighting. Daddy slaps Mommy and Mommy throws something at Daddy. I'm upstairs trying to keep my baby brother Stephen from crying.

This never happened, people.

And Brandon is barking his stupid puppy head off, and Daddy puts him in the backyard and everyone's fighting or crying so much that no one brings poor Brandon in and that night he gets loose and gets run over by a car.

Yeah, that sounds traumatic enough for a few more weeks.

It's like if you invent an interesting past, the dull boring one just goes away. All you need to do, really, is just believe your lies.

On some other Wednesday, I was losing my virginity to a babysitter. She steals my virginity on my parent's sofa in front of MTV playing some eighties hair band video.

Again, this never happened.

Oh sure, I say I remember feeling confused. I say I remember that dirty feeling I had. I say I remember feeling let down by sex. Being used.

My point is I say I remember a lot of things that I know didn't happen.

This is total immersion free association therapy. This is the wave of the future. By making up things, I tell myself, my therapist can truly figure out my underlying problems. By lying about sex, he can tell I have commitment issues. Or maybe I need attention.

There's a method to my madness. I'm not just lying to him out of boredom.

Do I ever have mood swings?

Sure, why not?

Suffer from bouts of depression that last for more than a couple of days?

Yeah, I can pencil that in for you. No problem.

Ever have panic attacks?

Only when I'm supposed to.

I tell him all about how I get scared when I'm in open public places. Walking through a park, I say, is pure hell for me. My palms get all sweaty and I get dizzy.

This is so not true that it's funny. And the really funny thing is that at my next session, he wants to discuss medication.

14

Brian and I are walking out of the pool hall a few blocks from his bookstore, heading to a bar for a few post-game brews. We're talking about is this weekend. What we're doing. Where we'll be. Who's going to drive. Planning is what most people call it.

Just as we get outside I hear someone call out, "Mr. Meridan? Is that you?"

A fan. An autograph seeker. One of my loyal audience members.

I turn around and face the fan, my autograph seeker. She's all wide eyed, but there's no paper in her hand. No pen. There's nothing at all.

"I've been looking all over for you!" Her words tumble out breathlessly. "You weren't at your gym yesterday like you usually are."

Oh, you're a member?

"Nope."

Oh, ok. Then you just happen to know when and where I work out. Cool.

"I've just been trying to get a hold of you, but I had to work up the nerve to talk to you. But it's not like I'm a stalker or anything. In fact, I'm one of your biggest fans, but I bet you hear that every day, huh? That I'm your biggest fan, I mean."

Isn't that the same thing the guy who shot Selena said?

"Yeah, so I just wanted to say hi, you know, polite and all."

"Well, ok, hi. Pleasure to meet you. Now, I have to be going."

"It's just that I've been trying to reach you at your office but your secretary, well, she's not the nicest rose on the bush if you know what I'm saying. I'll bet you haven't even got the messages I've been leaving. I left you my work number, my home number, my cell number, even my email address. You didn't get any of it, did you? I just knew it. Does Sara ring a bell? Sara Fisher?"

I can hear Eminem's *Stan* in my mind right now.

Brian is laughing so hard, I think he may fall over.

"Sometimes she gets busy. Lots of things on her plate, it's a busy place, as I'm sure you can imagine. Now, I must be going."

"It's just that I'm getting married, I think I told you that before when we talked."

She starts wringing her hands and shuffling towards me.

"I was just hoping you could make extra sure it doesn't rain that weekend, my parents are flying in from Florida and it's such an expensive event and all." She turns to Brian. "What are you laughing at?"

"Lady, do you really think *he* controls the weather? He *tells* you the weather, he doesn't *dictate* it. This dude, he can't dictate a memo."

"Are you, are you *kidding* me? Do you remember that guy, he was weatherman in the eighties, the guy with the toupee?"

Mitch Steiner. Yeah, I remember him.

"Well, he screwed up every other weekend. He'd say it was going to rain so you'd cancel your trip to the countryside, to pick berries or whatever, and it would be beautiful. But if he said it would be nice, guess what?" She looks at me like this is an obvious question.

It would rain?

"Exactly. See, you *do* remember him. But William here, he's a genius. A true miracle worker. If I was the Pope, he'd be a saint", she adds.

Being a saint means I'm dead. Awkward.

Even as I get into my car, she's still talking. I roll my windows all the way up, lock the doors, and she's still rambling on about her wedding.

And as I speed off, I look in the rear view mirror and it's not like I can read lips or anything, but I could swear she said she loves me.

■ ■ ■

I am at lunch with Neil on a Thursday. He is with a guy who worked over in R&D, and this is the first time I met Josh.

Josh was wearing a tie which he so eloquently pointed out was hieroglyphics for "wine them, dine them, sixty-nine them", which doesn't seem historically accurate to me. Neil looked pretty tired. He said he was at an art opening last night, over by Chinatown. I told him my brother had been at some art thingy yesterday, did he know a Stephen Meridan?

No, no, he assured me. There were so many people there, he couldn't even talk to a fraction of them if he wanted to.

Neil told me that Josh was planning on starting a boy band and calling them "The Hot Dudes". He was ready to write all the songs and coordinate all the dancing. Now all he needs is to find the talented lads.

I'm not thinking Pedophilia but I can't blame you if you were.

Always the glutton for punishment, I asked Josh if he had written any songs yet. He told me that he was working on a song titled "John Gotti". He had the refrain written already. It went "Pimp it, pimp it, work dat body. Work that thang like a young John Gotti". It was destined for greatness, he told me. He was going to sample the riff from the theme song from the old black and white "*The Untouchables*" television program.

"Did *The Untouchables* even have a theme song?" I inquired. Josh adamantly repeated his plan.

If you say it twice, it must be true, right?

Neil seemed rather amused by all this. I just kept waiting for Josh to fart and then giggle uncontrollably. He looked like he hadn't shaved in weeks, but he still had peach fuzz. He was drinking chocolate milk and eating a bologna sandwich with the crusts cut off.

This guy has got to be a mirage. He can't be sitting here. Josh can't exist. This guy is definitely a little bit off, but he's off in the right direction.

Josh finished his sandwich and gets up. As he's shaking my hand with the same cadence I jerk off to he says he and Neil are going to see the new Farlley brothers movie tonight, did I want to come?

I wouldn't miss it for the world.

I go back upstairs to my office and Megan tells me my father called a minute ago and please call him back. I sat behind my desk and called my father back, just as any good son would do. I got his secretary and chatted with her for a few minutes and then she put me through to my father. He wanted to know if I remembered my mother's birthday. Sure, I tell him, I did. Five months ago, you know, when it took place.

"Well, I know something is coming up. What is it? An anniversary?"

No, dad, that's in May. And he only had 38 years to get this down.

"Well, I know something is coming up. August 2, August 3, August 5, maybe? What's coming up, Billy?"

"Dad, your vacation is next week." Sigh.

"Ah yes, that's it. Vacation. Say, you coming down this year?"

Hmmm, a week with my mother and father. I'm going to have to pass on this one, Monty. I'll take what's behind door number two, thank you.

I told him I couldn't make it this year, what with all the time I just took off for my honeymoon.

"I thought you didn't marry Maryanne." Somewhere, a light bulb dimly flickers.

Monica. And I didn't.

With parental influence like this, is it any wonder I can't even take care of a fish?

15

I don't want you to mistake my apparent callousness and general negativity as the backbone of my character. I was a totally normal person. I was a dependable worker, a loving son and brother, yadda yadda yadda. I was normal. I am just not normal right now.

There is no way I'm normal right now.

Monica is the three hundred and forty-seventh most downloaded person on the Internet. Three forty-six is RuPaul. I suppose I should take pride in the fact my ex is more popular that a drag queen.

Three forty-eight is a woman weighing over three hundred pounds, bound and gagged, with "bitch" and "cunt" written all over her in lipstick. And she's wearing a gas mask. One really has to wonder *normal* is, exactly.

If I was normal, more people would want to make laws about how movie trailers go on. And on.

And on.

If I became the normal, they wouldn't sell beer in 24 ounce cans. If I became the normal, more people would have conversations with themselves. Normal people brush their teeth daily.

Normal is a retirement account, annual vacation. Normal is telling your kids to not do what you did as a kid. Normal is a picket fence and two cats and a dog and an SUV. Normal is knowing a gay person, but not being friends with one.

Before Monica filmed her sexual prowess, I ran a pretty normal life. I used to teat hree servings of fruit a day and I voted in most national elections. I got six hours of sleep a night. I could maintain eye contact with people. I used to bathe. I even had goals and ambition.

No, really, I did.

That is gone right now. I have none of that emotional stability anymore. That mental security. Sure, someday, it may come back to me, encircle me and keep me warm and cozy again, but I'm not holding my breath.

I don't blame Monica for this. No, she's just the reason it didn't happen earlier. I am the root cause. I ignored the obvious. Donned those rose-colored glasses with enthusiasm. I am the one who preferred my own padded world view and status quo and tradition. I simply managed to avoid culpability for my emotions. I allowed them to get sucked back and forth wherever. If I found a place that was easy to remain in, I just stayed put. It was much, much easier that way. Everything was laid out in front of me.

Boom, high school.

Boom, virginity gone.

Boom, college.

Boom, a job.

Boom, a wife.

Boom, kids.

Boom, retirement.

I guess I got derailed around wife.

What is an ex-girlfriend anyway? She's just a person after all. She doesn't have any magical powers. She can't do anything to me anymore unless I let her. My therapist told me that.

It's not like I think about Monica much anymore. Of course, it's not like I think much anymore period. Even if I try to, my brain just clicks off. Zip. My therapist tells me this is another defense mechanism. Funny how they seem to further separate you from reality, which was what caused the problem in the first place.

16

It was in an Uber with a Mexican driver named Pablo that Neil and Josh pull up to my curb around seven. I got in and greeted everyone. They were in the middle of a conversation and all I could put together was that Neil thought the subject of their debate was retarded in a big way while Josh thought there was a huge market for it..

"What you guys are talking about", I ask.

"I'm going to be a white rapper," Josh says. He said it with the sincerity one would say their own name. He bobbed his head a wee bit, making you believe a little more.

"A white rapper? You've got the white part down pat, but it's that second part you might be lacking?"

But no. Josh says it's all about attitude. All you need, he tells us, is a big hit, then exit stage left with the money. You don't stick around, and definitely no comeback tour, especially as a metal act.

Oh no, this was strictly a one time thing, not a career.

So what would Josh name himself?

"The Project, man, The Project."

"That's the understatement of the year right there," Neil muttered before turning to gaze out the window.

On the way to the theatre, Josh continued to outline his master plan on The Project's going platinum. It sounded pretty good, except for one thing.

Reality. Josh admittedly can't rap. He's never even listened to much rap. One could say that Josh lacked street cred.

I'm not thinking Pushing a Bag of Wonder Bread Through a Screen Door but I can't blame you if you were.

Still, he did have some bold ideas.

First, he wanted to have a black guy and a white girl in the group. He wanted the girl to be "some sort of fucking Britney-Spears-16-year-old who we can get to have her tits done, tonsils removed and get some cock sucking lips." Josh is a national treasure.

Second, no touring. Fake everything in the studio. This way, Josh wouldn't need to rap. You can just get someone else to do that. He just wanted to be part of the machine. Get his face on an album cover and say "hell yeah, bitches" on the album. He also wanted to be in a few videos with bouncing cars, Dobermans, and girls shaking their asses in front of the camera. Oh, and there had to be forties of malt liquor. It's 1989 all over again.

Third, life-like action dolls. These things sell, Josh reminds us, they sell big. Those Spice Girl dolls blew off the shelves a few decades ago. All the boy bands had them. And so would Josh.

We arrived at the theatre and got in line for tickets. We were herded to the bathroom. We followed the Judas Cow to the theatre.

I'm not thinking Cattle but I can't blame you if you were.

The movie was almost hilarious and afterwards, we got a cab and returned home. Brian called while I was at the movie so I called back. He wanted to know if I wanted to grab a few beers the next day. I told him I had a doctor's appointment, but I'd meet him at Skibble's afterwords.

■ ■ ■

After work I went to my therapist. It's Wednesday, you know.

He asked if I had gotten outrageously angry lately. I gladly told him that I had not. I told him I hadn't had any extreme emotions lately.

That's to be expected, he tells me, for a while. I was emotionally drained and it takes awhile for the good old emotional battery to recharge.

No, really. He said "the good old emotional battery."

He asked if I had been thinking about Monica much. I said a little here and there. Mostly when I am alone, mostly late at night when I can't sleep.

It's that I get lonely, I tell him, and I guess I blame that on Monica. She's supposed to be sleeping next to me, probably with some other guy's cum all crusty on her thigh.

But I don't say the other guy's cum part. I want to look good in front of my therapist. You know, a true gentleman.

He validates my feelings. I make sense in here. I follow obvious emotional patterns. Patterns of normalcy. Patterns of a uniform nature. I am so totally straight out of a textbook it's not even funny.

He asks me about my relationship with my parents. I tell him my mother is convinced I'm still a teenager and my father hasn't paid attention much since I was. All in all, they're good people who I love very much, but we're not what you'd call friends by any stretch.

Was I loved and nurtured as a child?

Ok, we're still on my childhood today.

Between my parents, four aunts, five uncles and all of my grandparents, yes I was. I assure him I had a happy childhood.

He tells me most people think they had a happy childhood. He tells me that everyone is supposed to have a happy childhood so we all want to think we had a happy childhood, too. Most people, he tells me, have a merely adequate childhood, and quite a number of us had down right crappy childhoods rife with passive abuse and neglect.

And they just repress these memories?

He wants to know if I've ever repressed anything.

Nope. It's all out there.

Have my parents ever abused me?

My dad took me to a few operas. He was 30 minutes late picking me up at school once. My mom used to make me eat Brussel sprouts. Nope. No abuse. No neglect. Sorry, you need to find a different excuse.

Not that there's anything that needs an excuse, mind you.

He wants me to tell him about my earliest childhood memory. Didn't we figure that one out last week? You remember, the dog, Brandon, and my parents fighting.

And he just looks at me. Like I should have something to say. The same damn look my boss gave me.

"Well, William, we both know you made that episode up."

And what makes you say that?

"Well, you referred to yourself as William and your brother as Stephen, but your parents as Mommy and Daddy. If you were really under, you would have used either the names you did then, or the names you use now, but not a mix of them. It's called identity displacement. That and people who are regressed twenty years never realize they have to urinate now."

Busted.

"So why don't we start over?"

"You mean, like, telling the truth and stuff? I don't know if that's too appealing right now. This whole *honesty* thing doesn't seem like it would work." This vaguely feels like one of those defense mechanisms at work.

And he wants to know why. This asshole went to school for this and he wants to know why I don't want to open up.

Gee, I don't know, maybe because when you wear your heart on your sleeve, some asshole rips your arm and beats you with it?

"Ok then. How about your first real memory. Try this time. I'll even turn the white noise off."

But I have no clue what came first or what. There's no chronological order. All I can really remember is either being put in or taken out of car seats. I guess my childhood was a lot of car seats.

He wants to know what I usually think about when I'm trying to go to sleep. Usually, it's what I have to do the next day, making sure I didn't forget anything from the day, that sort of thing.

He wants to know if I ever get suicidal at night. I tell him I don't.

"Is that normal, too?" I ask.

He tells me that people who go through a traumatic experience like mine sometimes get suicidal at night. He tells me it's most likely a by-product of being alone and feeling vulnerable.

Can you tell me what *isn't* about being alone and feeling vulnerable?

He asks me if there's anything I'd like to tell him, to get off of my chest. He wants to know if there's a history of depression in my family.

"Why? Am I depressed?" Where did this come from?

"Well, you exhibit the signs; complacency, listlessness, no sense of purpose, covering things up, these sorts of things may indicate a bigger problem. But your time is up. We can discuss this next time."

I get up and slide out of the room without moving my feet.

■ ■ ■

After I left my therapist's, I head to Skibble's. Brian was there waiting. He had a beer and a shot lined up for both of us.

"So what did the doc say? Have cancer?"

"I wish. No, it was just a routine check up. He did a stress test. I'm fine. Nothing a few drinks can't fix, right?"

We sat idly for awhile. There was a hockey game on and the place was starting to fill up with people getting off work. We kept filling our empty glasses.

"Dude, do you remember that time I bet a double dime on the Notre Dame game?"

How could I forget? Back in our senior year of high school, Brian somehow got the phone number to some bookie. Convinced Notre Dame would beat Michigan, he called and bet a double dime on the game, thinking it was $20. Little did he know a dime meant a thousand dollars. And little did he know Michigan would kick Notre Dame's Catholic ass up and down the field.

When the bookie's "associates" called him to collect, he nearly had a heart attack. He called my house to see if he could borrow some cash, but I wasn't home. Stephen, who was friends with him too, lent him his savings, $355. When they found me, I lent him my savings, $200. This, coupled with Brian's $20, bought us an additional week to raise the money. Brian was reminded that a knee was worth a grand.

Faced with no chance to raise the almost $1500 we needed to keep Brian walking, we decided to donate blood plasma.

Twice a day. Every day.

This still didn't give us enough cash, so we decided to add sperm donations to our list of public services. It was a simple plan. Go to a blood bank and donate. Go to next blood bank and donate. Hit the sperm bank and jerk off.

We learned two lessons due to this: first, a dime meant a grand, and second, jerking off with only four quarts of blood in you isn't good for your health.

Our plan was ended when Brian passed out, dick in hand, at the sperm bank. We've been barred for life since.

"Yeah, I remember, dumb ass."

We sat quietly for awhile, drinking our beers and watching the game.

"So, found any new babes yet?" If looks could kill, Brian would be roadkill.

"Not yet. I still need more time to lick the wounds."

"Dude, you can't let one nymphomaniac stop you from your quest for both a healthy relationship and hot freaky circus monkey sex."

"I'm going to pass on sex with monkeys. Besides, there's no good looking women in here."

"Are you blind or something? Check the chick over by the pool table. Nice ass, cute face, and let's see, yep, a nice rack. Dude, I would kill a homeless man to feed off of those jugs. And her friend just went to the bathroom. Now is your time. You control your fate, Bill. You. Are. The. Man."

I must have been buzzed because I walked over. I know I initiated conversation, but I haven't the faintest as to what I said. Whatever it was, it must have worked. She smiled and introduced herself. Jennifer. We talked for a few minutes, me feigning interest in her job, her rambling about mine. Her friend came back and I ordered us a round. We kept talking and then she said her and her friend were off to meet some other friends at a club downtown. I asked for her phone number and she jotted ten digits on a napkin. She gave me a big bright smile and left.

I returned to Brian high as a kite. An atomic bomb could have gone off and I wouldn't have cared.

"The lion returns from the kill. How was the meal, Mr. King of the Jungle?"

"She didn't stand a chance." I was eight feet tall. I was the slayer of great dragons. I have a dick three feet long and eighty pound balls. I am all man all the time.

We spent some more time drinking and then we headed home. I had to be at work early tomorrow.

■ ■ ■

It was obvious I couldn't call her the next day. That would look way to pathetic and needy. Even if the girl is your soul mate, wait at least two days. Girls can smell desperation faster than a bloodhound in heat.

And of course, the only thing I could think about was calling her.

When I did call, I would need a plan. There was no room to ad lib. Women love that air of confidence. I'm not saying you tell her what you're going to do, but if you present the date in a clear and concise way, it's much harder to say no.

So what was the best course of action? Well, dinner always works, but you need something more. An event. Something to show what kind of guy you are.

If you want to be adventurous, go rock climbing. If you want to come off as playful, ride go carts. If you want athletic, play miniature golf and maybe drive a bucket of balls. If you want to be an intellectual, walk around a Barnes and Noble for an hour, sucking down expensive coffee and pretending to enjoy Ayn Rand's books. It's not that hard.

To fake it, I mean, not to enjoy Ayn Rand's books.

I call Megan into my office.

"Name a nice, romantic restaurant in the city."

"Are you asking me out? That's harassment. Sexual harassment. And you know I have a boyfriend."

Right. The fag.

"Ok. Um, it was for another girl, one I just met. Just asking a question. Sorry." She turned bright red and looked down at her shoes like they were works of art.

"Oops. Sorry about that. Jumped to a conclusion, huh? I've, um, been a little jumpy lately."

Sure, no problem. So where does your boyfriend take you, I ask her.

And she tells me Danny the Fag is flat ass broke. Well, she said Denny's, but we all know what that means. And she didn't say the fag part, either.

That was all me.

"Ok, if you can name a nice place, I'll spring for you two lovebirds to go. A summer bonus."

"Are you serious?" Her face lit up like the 4th of July. What, do all women expect men to lie? She did that half-squint/raise an eyebrow thing. Great, the tacit assumption all men lie.

"Well, Allophone's is a nice place. Dim but not dark, great pasta. Pricey, but not expensive. Good seafood."

I tell her to make a reservation for tomorrow around eight o'clock, and make one for her next week. She says ok and tells me that Stephen called a few hours ago and really needs to talk to me.

The last time Stephen "really had to talk to me", he had taken too much LSD and thought he was Jesus Christ as a Mormon, converting Native Americans while riding a dinosaur. The worst part was that it took him two weeks to get over this. Seriously, he even changed his name tag at work to "Savior".

So the only thing left was to call Jennifer and arrange that date. The next day at work I pulled her number out and dialed the digits. I took a deep breath and exhaled.

"Thank you for calling A Plus Singles Dating Service, how may I forward your call?"

"Um, Jennifer?" I asked, mumbling.

"Do you have a box number, sir?"

A box number?

"Are you a first time caller? If so- "I hung up. I closed my eyes. I screamed at the top of my lungs.

■ ■ ■

I'm thinking that gratification is overrated. I'm thinking that standards are ruining our nation. I'm thinking that my soul is a great void, devoid of anything good or beneficial.

I'm feeling like setting fire to a kindergarten. I'm feeling like opening fire in an emergency room. I'm thinking that the world owes me a whole lot of reparations. I am sitting in my living room with Brian.

Brian says I shouldn't hate all women just because one chick is a stupid fucking cunt.

I say if the shoe fits, throw it at her.

Brian says I need to calm down, I need to settle, I need to relax.

I say what I need is to slaughter a tauntaun and climb on it.

Brian says I'm overreacting. Brian says have a beer and chill, man. Brian thinks I'm acting like a lunatic. Brian says focus on the positive. He wants me to seek professional help. Brian says therapy.

If Brian only knew.

It's raining out and I want to go out to get some food but Brian thinks we should just order in. Chinese or pizza? These are the questions that shape our lives. Pepperoni or wonton soup? Life or death? Cat or dog?

My phone rings. Brian looks at me, waiting for me to answer it. I wave offhandedly, muttering something about "… you do it…" Brian picks it up. It's Stephen. I am not up for Stephen right now. I get up and walk out of the room.

I'm thinking that masturbation should be an Olympic event. I'm thinking that dental floss is a sound long term investment. I'm thinking the KY is still next to my toothpaste.

Brian tells me that Stephen *needs* to talk to me. Now.

I tell Brian that Stephen *needs* to suck a fat dick. I'm not talking on the phone today, I don't care if Joan of Arc calls offering hot phone sex. No. Fucking. Way.

Brian hangs up, telling Stephen I'd call later, that I was bummed over some girl.

A worthless vagina, I remind him, just a worthless vagina.

We order from the pizza place down the street. I order a cheesesteak, fried onions, bacon, and mayo. Brian gets a stromboli or something. I really couldn't care less at this point.

Brian is sitting on the end of my bed, talking to me even though I'm buried under both pillows. "Dude, you're acting like a freak, like some bull dyke on her first period. So some girl gave you a fake number. Big deal. There are other girls out there. She wasn't even that good looking. Her cheeks looked plastic. It might have been the makeup but I wouldn't take the chance, you know?" I moan, quiet at first, then louder and louder until Brian shuts up.

"Who even uses phone dating sites these days? We've got POF and CL M4W and OK Cupid if you want more than dirty, casual sex." This is what stung just as much as the rejection. This bitch strung me along with 1994 technology.

And what if I texted her? Huh? What then?

I'm thinking that roller derby is the answer to race re-lations. I'm thinking ATMs are churches and the Big Bang Theory explains David Lee Roth leaving Van Halen. The ac-tual theory, not the show.

I'm thinking like a guy on bath salts that thinks eating his own face is a good decision.

The food arrives and I don't eat it. I'm not hungry. I don't want, need or desire anything. I hereby renounce all earthly possessions. To protest the new world order, I throw my chees-esteak out the window. It just misses a black Lexus.

I feel like battery acid is coursing through my veins. My heart is pounding against my rib cage. My skin is so tight. Too tight. I feel the burn. I'm seconds away from erupting into a human torch

Brian tells me to get some sleep, he'll call me tomorrow.

What day is it, I ask.

"Saturday, chief. Get some rest."

■ ■ ■

The next morning, around 11:30, the phone rings. I'm just lying in bed thinking about whatever. I expect it to be Brian so I pick it up.

"May I please speak to William Meridan?"

"Oh Christ. You fuckers call on Sundays now? Look, take me off your God damn list and-"

"Sir, I'm calling from St. Mary's hospital. Your father has been in an accident."

Fucking great. Here's that pang of reality punching through thermal wrap of self-absorbed pity. No one expects their parents to die barring some announcement of a terminal disease or whatever. Cancer or something. Parents are the one constant on this planet. They raise you the best they can. They work hard. They retire. They become grandparents. They get old and then you shove them into a nursing home. You. Not them. Not God. You. No one walks your parents to the grave but you. That's the normal progression. I'm still on stage 2. They're working hard.

"What kind of accident?"

"Sir, there was a car crash. You should come down immediately."

The voice on the other end went away after the click and I hung up. I'm sitting here, on the edge of my bed for a few minutes, shaking with fear. I think this may be palsy. On the bright side, I'm not thinking of all the dudes Monica blew while we were together, so there's that. I pick up the phone and called Stephen.

"Stephen, its Bill. We need to go to the hospital. It's Dad."

"Bill? Great! I need to talk to you."

"Jackass, we need to go to the hospital. Dad was in an accident."

"First I need to tell you something. Bill, this is really important to me. Just listen."

"Asshole. Dad, car crash, hospital. Which part can't you understand? Get it together and grab a cab. I'll meet you there."

I got in my car. I don't remember getting in my car. I don't even remember driving on the highway, even though I was on it for 5 miles. All I remember was running up to the information desk.

The nurse tells me my father was being operated on as we speak. She says his condition was critical. She said Embolism. She said Brain Damage. She said a big word that was probably Latin but who the fuck knows? More fancy Latin-sounding words. Finally, she said to take a seat, a doctor would be with me as soon as possible.

I found a coffee machine next to the men's room and I used a swig of this vile diesel jet fuel coffee to wash down one of the Prozac my therapist gave me. My eyes were dry. I swallowed deeply and tried to relax.

I fucking hate hospitals.

I also hate fucking hospitals.

I was sitting with my head down when someone taps me on the shoulder and says, "Billy?"

I look up and there's my history teacher from my senior year, Mr. Liddicote. He was with a young boy, his son I guessed, who's arm was wrapped in a freshly minted cast. He told me his kid broke his arm sliding into second base head first.

A regular Charlie Hustle.

And he asks me why I'm here.

Because I apparently owe Satan money or something. Because I got my dick mangled in an electric can opener. Why do you think I'm in an emergency room? Because stupidity like this guy has should be painful.

"My dad was in a car crash."

The asshole looks at me, and while patting his jerk-off-waste-of-food kid, says with a huge shit-eating grin, "That's too bad. Best of luck there. But what are the odds? My son, your dad, same hospital."

Yeah, it's a small world and getting smaller all the time.

17

I had been sitting there for twenty minutes when I saw Stephen come through the door. He looked around the ward, quite confused. To the best of my knowledge, Stephen has never been conscious in an emergency room.

As I was waiting for Stephen to pick through the many faces in the waiting area – all four of us – to determine which one was me, there was a tap on my shoulder.

"William Meridian?" asked a lanky guy wearing one of those green nurses outfits, whatever they're called, with a surgical mask hanging from his neck. He was young and his eyes lit up as I turned to regard him. I've been on TV.

"Yeah?"

"It's a pleasure to meet you. I'm Doctor Duncan."

Yeah it *is* a pleasure, motherfucker. How's my fucking dad? Instead I say, "Likewise. What's news on my dad?" It's then that I noticed the damp red stain on his right sleeve and my stomach clenched.

He drew a practiced breath and motioned for me to sit down. I sighed. You don't spend your days on TV without learning to spot an act. I could be pissed, but right now I just needed to play along and get to the part about Dad.

"I'm sorry." He said. And that's all he said. I don't fucking remember the rest. I guess it was something like, "Your dad passed away a little while ago."

"Passed... away?" Like, no more Dad? Not brain damage. Just fucking nothing.

"By the time he arrived," Dr. Duncan continued, "there was little we could do. He was in a severe state of hemorrhagic shock. Unresponsive. Multi-organ failure. He'd been hypoxic for too long."

"There had to be something you could've..."

The Doctor's sympathetic smile faded a bit and the act faltered. They didn't like being accused. "William, the cranial injuries your father sustained alone were sufficiently fatal. Couple that with the polytrauma to the body and unchecked internal bleeding, there was no chance. Even a massive transfusion of fresh blood would've been like pouring it down the drain. The body had already given out." By now Stephen had found me.

"Bill, what's going on?"

"Shit, Stephen, Dad just died."

"What the fuck? Oh man. Oh man. Fuck. How? How did it happen?"

"Car crash. Doctor, do you know any details about the crash? I mean he never sped, he always wore his seatbelts. Fuck, his car had so many damn air bags you could float it across a river. What happened?"

"Yes, there was a Veronica Martin in the car as well. She died on impact. Her head was crushed by the steering wheel."

He gave us this look that said this should answer any of our questions.

"Was she driving? Dad never let anyone drive his car. Hell, I had to rent a car to take my driver's test. The man never rode shotgun in his life."

"Who's Veronica, Bill?" Ladies and gentlemen, I give you my brother.

"She *was* Dad's secretary." This is way too much.

"No, to the best of my knowledge, he was driving." I can see the doctor flinch as he says this.

"Then how did she get killed by the steering wheel? Side impact? What?"

"Well, the paramedics believe she was... well... umm... fellating him, but there's no police report yet."

"Dude, Bill, what's that mean?" I can tell Stephen's brain is working overtime due to the furrows in his brow.

"To fellate someone." Emptiness is his eyes. "Fellatio." Naïve innocence. "It's a fucking blowjob, retard. Veronica was sucking Dad off."

"Dad died getting roadhead?" It's like the obituary writes itself.

I turned back to Dr. Duncan. "How can you be sure?" This has to be a sick, sick joke.

"During on scene efforts to resuscitate Ms. Martin, they cleared a rather large bolus of ejaculate from her airway." He stopped and broke eye contact for just a moment. Was he stifling a laugh? No. It couldn't be. He's a fucking professional and this shouldn't phase him. "Additionally," he continued, "it was evident that her jaw seized up upon impact..."

I didn't listen to the rest. No man should ever have to hear about his father's genitals. But the damage was done. Dad died without a dick.

"Can you reattach it?" asked Stephen with an intense look.

I'm damn sure the Hippocratic oath says, Thou shalt not laugh. But of course Dr. Duncan blew a gob of snot right onto the floor and then tried to pass it off as a quick coughing fit.

"The police aren't done with their investigation yet and I'm sure they'll want to talk to you, but it appears as if your father lost control as he climaxed. I heard there aren't any skid marks in front of the building."

"What building?"

"Oh. He ran into St. Jude's Religious Store on Fifth and Mandrane."

So my Dad was dead. Deceased. No longer among the living. My father had kicked that troublesome oxygen habit. He was past tense. History.

I wanted to disappear. I wanted to go away, into a cocoon.

But losing my father wasn't enough. Oh no. I was Job and Stephen was the Old Testament God and this doctor was Satan and they were going to see just how much they could dump on me before I took hostages.

Just when everything couldn't possibly get worse, Stephen told me what he has been dying to tell me for days.

"Bill, I'm going to Hawaii in two weeks to get married."

Dazed from all of this, I looked at him and said, "Uhh great. Wow. Uhh. Married? You? *Married*? Who's the girl and why the fucking fuck are you bringing this up right now?"

"Well, that's why we're going to Hawaii. I'm, um, not marrying a girl. I'm marrying Neil Zuelig. You know him, you work with him."

Dad dies dickless after being blown by his nineteen-year-old secretary and ten minutes later my kid brother tells me he's gay. Oh, and marrying my co-worker. My fiancée and I broke up over her vagina which apparently issues frequent flyer miles. Girls I try to pick up refer me to a dating service. I think I may exhibit signs of male pattern baldness. My therapist wants to up me to three times a week counseling. Some freak thinks I control the weather for her wedding.

This is my life.

■ ■ ■

"Men ejaculate in your colon? And you *like* it? Oh my God." Stephen looked at me like a kicked puppy. Love and support, love and support. I got this. I'm granite. "You. Get. Sodomized." I sat down, putting my forehead in my hands.

"You're not being fair to your brother. One shouldn't be made to feel guilty over their sexual preferences." Why the hell is an old high school teacher preaching to me when his jerkwad son could obviously use an ass kicking.

I rise again and face my brother. The teacher is to my left. I refuse to look at him.

"And how long have you been gay? A few hours now? Maybe even a whole *freaking* weekend? What is it? I remember you with girls. Hot girls. When did this happen? Are you get-drunk-and-let-a-guy-blow-you gay or getting-your-ass-reamed-by-a-thirteen-inch-cock gay?"

"I'm just regular gay. I've, I've always been this way. Since I can remember I liked boys. Sure, I pretended to like girls, and there's nothing really wrong with them, but I like to sleep with men. Neil, in particular. Sorry."

"You're God damn right you're sorry."

The teacher puts a hand on my shoulder and I brush it away.

"Why in the world are you telling me this now? What, is it written somewhere that in the event of Dad's death you reveal your homosexuality? Is that it? Why not last year? Why not in high school?"

"Because I wasn't ready then. I wasn't ready until now. Not until Neil and I decided to settle down and commit to each other."

"And just how long have you been with Neil", I ask him. "Is this why he's been nice to me?"

"We've been dating for two years now. And he's nice to you because he thinks you're a nice guy. And he's a nice guy. I mean, he thought you'd kill him if you found out about us."

"And what's this about marriage?"

"We got engaged last week."

"And who got down on their knee?"

"That would be me." My brother, the true romantic.

I turn to the doctor. "I knew it. I just did. He's my kid brother after all." I turn back to Stephen.

"Do you realize our father died *getting* a blowjob?"

Yes, he does.

"Do you realize you're just as likely to die *giving* a blowjob? Do you?" Some random woman who I hadn't seen as of yet decided to intervene.

"You know, oral sex is a normal and natural part of a person's sexuality. Even with homosexuals."

"May I ask why you're here? Ok, my dad is dead, my brother is gay, you are not really needed in this fucking situation."

"Well, I am truly sorry. I was trying to enlighten a heathen who is attempting to make a pariah out of his brother. This isn't easy for him you know."

"Consider me enlightened." I wave my hand behind the woman, indicating her best path of retreat. This bitch in front of me and me without live ammunition.

She stared at me for a few moments and then turned and left. I looked back at my brother. He looked pretty upset. He looked shell shocked. I knew I was being rough on him but this is just more than my mind can respond to.

This is sensory overload.

This is looking into a mirror on too much acid.

This is a meltdown. This is Armageddon.

This is the apocalypse.

18

Three days later, two hundred people showed up at my father's viewing. There were lots of family and people my father worked with. And there were plenty of people I have never seen in my life. At least a handful are just here for the free buffet, for sure.

My mother arrived- fashionably late as always- with a strange man on her arm. As soon as she saw me, she came right over. "William, meet Jerry. Jerry, William." We shook hands and made idle talk for a few moments until my mother asked Jerry to get her a cup of coffee.

"Mom, who's that?"

"William, your eyes look terrible. Are you taking your zinc supplement?"

"Mom. Who is that guy?"

"Oh, Jerry? He's my boyfriend."

"Your *boyfriend*? Um, Dad's not even buried yet. His body is right over there. You should have what my shrink would call *healing time*." I point to the casket.

"Oh, Nathan knew about him. William, your father and I had an open relationship."

Yeah, open like Monica's legs.

"William, see the woman over there? That's Amanda, his girlfriend." She waves at her and the woman waves back.

My mother goes on to tell me that her and my father hadn't had sex since Stephen was born. Sure, they loved each other, but they weren't *in* love with each other. In fact, they really couldn't stand each other. She tells me they stayed together for the children. That, and divorces are expensive. She tells me that when they were younger, they used to go to swinger parties.

If my mom was a swinger, then how didn't she know what K-Y Jelly is?

Oh sweet Jesus, my mother is a sexual well-oiled catcher's mitt. *Shudder.*

My mother tells me she knows about the whole Veronica thing. She knows my father died being gobbled like a Thanksgiving turkey. She doesn't care much. By now Jerry has returned. I can't stand to be near him, so I excuse myself.

Brian walks up behind me and says, "Sorry, dude."

"Brian, did you hear that Stephen's gay? And engaged?"

"No, but I figured he was gay."

"Huh?"

"Yeah, dude, you couldn't tell? Dude, he hums Broadway show tunes for crying out loud. I thought he was gay since high school."

"No way, I tell him. Since high school?"

"Dude, do you remember his senior prom date?" Yeah. So?

"Bill, she was a hardcore dyke. I mean *hardcore*."

No way, I tell him. She wasn't a lesbian.

"Dude, the only thing that's munched more beaver than her is a mountain lion. I mean, she was going to college to study Women's Studies. Women's Studies, dude, Women's fucking Studies. That'd be like me getting a PhD in the D, you know?"

So everyone knew my brother was gay but me. My parents didn't sleep with each other, but at least they were friendly with their spouse's dates. And then who walks through the door?

Monica.

Porn star Monica.

Monthly HIV tests Monica.

Maybe you remember her. I can't seem to forget her.

"What the hell are you doing here? This is my father's viewing. What are you doing here?"

"William, I was close to your father, you know."

Hey, she's close with a lot of people, if you get my drift.

"But he's my father," I whisper under my breath. "Not yours. This is awkward for me. So you shouldn't be here."

What I mean is, I say, let me grieve. I can't mourn my father when I'm looking at the face that's sucked a million dicks.

"You ruined my bachelor party, isn't that enough?" Not to mention marriage but I find that kind of irrelevant here.

She rolls her eyes. "You make it sound as if that was my intention. Why is everything about you? Who made you the center of the universe, Copernicus?"

"Um, Copernicus proved the opposite."

"Stop being a little lawyer. Why must you nit pick every-thing with me? You get my point. Look, let me say good bye to Nathan and I'll leave you alone forever, I swear. For a guy barely packing five inches, you sure as hell act important."

Gee, sorry I'm not hung like a rhino and making porn.

I'm not thinking Fragile Male Ego but I can't blame you if you were.

I walk over to a seat and sit down. I get up and get a cup of coffee. People keep coming up to me, offering me their condo-lences as if it will bring my father back to life. Like pity is Dr. Frankenstein himself. They all say, "We're so sorry to hear of your father's passing."

Or, "This was so unexpected."

Or, "What a tragedy this is."

Yeah, I know. You don't have to tell me about it. If you think this is bad for you, imagine how I feel. As if I expect these people to be joyous about the situation.

Stephen walks up to me and gives me a hug. He says, "You know Neil." Neil shakes my hand while looking down.

"Neil, how's it going?"

"Oh, fine." Still looking down

"I'm not going to kill you, you know. I'm not mad at you or anything."

"Oh, ok." Still looking down.

"Stephen, I wanted to apologize for all the things I said at the hospital. I totally overreacted. It must have been Dad, you know? Anyway, I'm cool with the whole "gay" thing. So, I guess congratulations are in order."

Neil looks confused. I'm guessing Stephen didn't tell him the full version of our hospital conversation.

We talk for a little bit longer and then the ceremony begins.

■ ■ ■

Afterwards, we proceed to the graveyard where the funeral was to take place. Thankfully, Monica didn't follow. I didn't want two dead bodies.

The priest began his eulogy. Everyone sat in silence while he told us how this is a man being taken before his time. How we should focus on his life, not his death.

Yeah, it's probably best to not mention the fatal blowjob where he blew his load like a dog sneezing causing him to lose control of the car and crashed into the religious causing a shit load of damage.

The priest keeps right on going. About twenty minutes into his speech, I look over and there's my father's brother, my Uncle Alan, taking a leak on a tombstone. As nonchalantly as possible, I get up and walk over to him. Before I even get within ten feet, I can smell the whiskey.

"Uncle Alan, what are you doing? You can get arrested for this. You'd best zip up. For Christ's sake, this is a funeral, not a bar."

"Billy, you were always a good lad. Help unscrew this flask. It's stuck."

No, it's not stuck, you're tanked.

I take his flask and slip it in my pocket. I tell him that's he's had enough. He'd better just sit down.

"Don't you dare tell me what to do. I fought those lousy Viet Kong to keep my rights, I'm not having some God damned liberal fag brat tell me what to do."

I'm not the gay one but thanks.

You're making a scene, I tell him. Settle down.

He says, "Listen, Billy, you'd better give that back or I'll kick your ass" but he's so hammered it sounds like, "Lishen, Billy, you'd bedder give that bach or I'll kiss your ash."

And when I tell him he's not getting it back, he takes a swing at me.

And he misses. And he falls over.

And he hits a tombstone.

There's blood everywhere and everyone's looking and all I can do is say, "Its ok. Everything is under of control."

Everyone's eyes are on me and all I can do is stare at my passed out uncle, blood pouring from a gash on his forehead, and zipper down.

So let's recap.

My ex-fiancée is a porn star.

My boss forced me into therapy.

My brother is gay and marring my co-worker.

My father died dickless, getting blown by a mistress who wasn't even his girlfriend.

My mother could care less about this because now her social calendar opened right up.

My uncle is passed out in a graveyard with his dick hanging out.

Well, if you think this is a regular downward spiral of humanity, you'd better stop reading right now. Seriously. Plant a tree or something. Call your mother. Because this is nowhere near rock bottom. It gets worse, I swear. Much worse. Your local community college offers a wide range of classes that are both educational and practical. Seriously, you should stop reading and do that.

They say you don't know the bottom until you rebound from it. But there's no rebound in sight here. Trust me on this.

All I'm saying here is I didn't ask for this.

I didn't ask for my father to die or my brother to be gay or my mother to be a swinger or whatever. And I didn't ask to be a celebrity either.

19

I'm bored on a Saturday night so I'm watching some Big Ten football game on ESPN when my phone rings. It's my producer, asking me if I'm watching the station.

Nope, I tell him, Iowa at Wisconsin. Why?

"Switch the damn channel. Now!"

I turn it on and there's Paul, live outside some reception hall or something, getting poured on. Man, the rain was really coming down. Good, let him suffer, the little bitch.

"Ok. So Paul's getting rained on. So?"

"Moron, do you have the volume up? Are you listening to what the man is saying?" Like it really matters what words are coming out of his mouth, but I turn it up anyway.

"…only two of the hostages have managed to escape *Riberto's* and they describe quite a gristly scene…"

"What the fuck is Paul talking about?"

"…an estimated two hundred people are being held at gunpoint, two, possibly three handguns and at least one shotgun, by a disgruntled newlywed, one Sara Fisher. It seems as if her rants are aimed at one in our family…"

Just wait one god damned minute here. I know that name. I know her. She's the crazy chick. This doesn't feel good.

"... our very own diligent weatherman, William Meridan. From early reports, it appears as if she blames William for the rain today. She seems focused on shortcomings in William's meteorological prowess and those two witnesses said..."

That fucker has been waiting to take shots at my meteorological prowess for years, I bet.

I'm sitting there, staring blankly at the screen. My producer is definitely saying something right now. All I can do is watch Paul's lips move, oblivious to the actual words.

"This isn't good," I hear as I tune back into the phone conversation. "This is bad press. All the other stations are covering this, too." I flip through the other networks, and there's the same parking lot in the rain with flashing red lights. Great.

"... hold one, just a second, I think I heard gunfire. Six shots, at least..."

Even through the TV, I can hear the shots ring out. I can hear the people inside scream. Then, just when it gets really, really silent, that weird kind where the silence actually gets loud, there's this shot that sounds loud as shit, and really loud screaming. The cameraman must have slipped or dropped his camera because it's sideways now. I flip to other stations, but they don't have squat either.

"Well, William, I think it's clear we're going to need to have a meeting tomorrow morning. This is bad press. We can't have that. Be in my office at seven. Good night."

Paul is back on the screen. He is wide eyed and waving his hands furiously around while he speaks. This guy is such a douche bag.

"… reports of eight killed, including the gun man, I mean gun *woman*, and another twelve wounded…"

This is why no one watches the news anymore.

I'm not thinking Golden Age of Radio but I can't blame you if you were.

A few clicks over, CNN has the same feed.

Paul, rambling on about dead people, hostages he keeps calling them, but all I can hear, over and over again is my name.

William Meridan.

Our weather man.

William motherfucking *Meridan.*

■ ■ ■

The next morning, after a night of suck-ass sleep, I arrive at work to find camera crews camped out the parking lot. I'm not even out of my car when there's a mic thrust in front of me along with an onslaught of questions.

What do I think about the events of last night?

How do I feel about these tragic events?

What I want to know is why are the other stations covering this?

After repeating "no comment" thirty or forty times, I finally get inside. Every one was staring at me, just like at my bachelor party. All eyes are on me.

No one is saying a word.

People hush up as I walk by, lips drawn and eyes down until I'm past them.

All I can think about is how many of these people have watched Monica screw some guy? How many have seen her give head, like *really* suck a cock?

I walk around the corner and there are three guys from Receiving and I *just* know they've seen her movies.

"Ass-alicious 3: Bad to the Boner" or "Dark Meat X-travaganza", it doesn't matter to me. They have to know my ex-fiancé is a porn star or at the very least that I drove a crazed woman to kill her new husband.

The things I do to weddings, you know. Fuck me.

I go straight past my office and head to my producer's. His secretary smiles widely as she buzzes me in. I head straight into his office and close the door.

"Bill. There's ten dead. Twelve more wounded. She named you. You *personally*. It looks bad for the station. Our weather man drives 'em crazy, literally."

Has he seen Monica muff dive? Take it in the back door?

"The decision is out of my hands."

I can see his hands. Pumping two squirts of hand lotion into his palms and lubing up his cock. Staring at her tits and stroking, stroking, stroking.

He's saying something about severance pay but I see him naked, sitting in his leather recliner, jerking off to my ex-fiancé. There's little beads of perspiration on his forehead, and with his left hands, he's rubbing his nuts raw.

He keeps muttering things under his breath. Vile things. And after three minutes, he finally holds his breath and shoots all over his stomach.

"It's not like I didn't go to bat for you, but…"

And I know he doesn't wash his hands off. Oh no, this pervert right here, this little masturbator, this one-man love making crew, he just rubs his cum in. I can see his Mormon Trail getting all sticky and he just puts his shirt back on.

So when he says that it's been good working with me and he values me as a co-worker, and extends his hand for a firm shake, it's not that hard to look at him weird and say "Who the fuck are you kidding?"

■ ■ ■

Let's just jump to the part where I leave the building. Cleaning out my office? Not important. Saying good bye to Megan? Nope. Flipping Paul off and calling him a cock smoking fag-boy, while personally gratifying, doesn't do a thing to advance the narrative here. It's all about Kyle Wennington.

I go back out to my car only to find the camera crews have stayed. Their vans have my car boxed in. I'm screaming for them to move out of my way while saying "No comment" over and over again.

What is the station's official stance on last night's events?

How will I handle the trauma of last night's events?

How will I mourn for these dead people I don't even know?

What do I do, start a GoFundMe site? For the families of the victims? What about the survivors? GoFuckMe.

That's when a hand lands on my shoulder and I hear a deep, confidant voice say that Mr. Meridan has no comment at this time but will schedule a press conference later in the week. That the events of last night are a tragedy and we should focus on the families of the lost. The hand on my shoulder turns me around and there's a limo waiting with its door open. The hand pushes me inside, gets inside after me and closes the door.

The body that the hand belongs to is handsome. His hair is slicked back and his tortoise shell glasses look like they cost a couple of hundred dollars, or more.

"My name is Kyle Wennington, and I'm your agent."

I don't have an agent.

"You'll need one. Actually, right there, you needed one."

Yeah, well, I could have taken care of that myself.

"Sure. Famous last words. Anyway, we have a meeting in two hours with this production company. They're pretty excited about the possibilities of your show."

Show? What show?

"Oh, you can catch up at the meeting. It's no biggie. Now, which sounds better: John Sterling or Todd Powers?"

Huh? I'm so out of this conversation it's not funny.

"Your new working name."

What's wrong with my name?

"Come on now. You're partly responsible for a dozen deaths."

But I didn't kill those people. It was some crazed woman.

"I know that. You know that, but Joe Six-pack, he knows jack shit about reality. He knows what I tell him he knows."

So tell him I didn't kill those people. It's, what do they call it? Oh yeah, the *truth*.

"It doesn't work like that. You were in news, I thought you knew all about this stuff."

This is how I became John Sterling. God, I'm so fucking stupid.

STATION BREAK

Barbie Hudson: So, Mike, how does it feel to be the new weatherman on the News Tonight Team?

Mike Jensen: Barbie, this is a dream come true, you know? Great city, great people, and a great team. I'm looking forward to getting on air, and Paul from sports... he's been giving me the 411 on what goes on around here.

BH: Paul sure is a great guy. So tell us about your time in Omaha.

MJ: Well, first of all, Omaha is a great city. I just loved Nebraska. The people were down to earth and the spring and summer were gorgeous...

BH: Sounds like there's more to that sentence! (laughing)

MJ: (laughing) Well, yeah. It gets cold there. I don't love the cold, but my fiancé doesn't like the cold one bit.

BH: Fiancé? Well, that's... a... great news?

{Four seconds of silence}

BH: So where are you from, Mike? News crews tend to be a group of wanderers...

MJ: (interrupting)... nomads!

BH: Right. Nomads.

MJ: Well Barbie, I was born outside of Portland, Oregon, but was raised a little bit of everywhere. My dad was in the Air Force so the nomadic lifestyle is something I'd become used used to at a young age. By the time I left for college in Florida- again, no fan of the cold- I'd lived in nine different states and never for longer than-

BH: Well, Mike, I'm getting that hand gesture off camera. {Both laugh} Time to pay those bills. We'll be back in 120 seconds for more with Channel Seven's new weatherman, Mike Jensen.

20

In the future, man will no longer need constant affection to survive. In the future, there will be more communication on a personal level. In the future children will always be reminded they are special and adults will always be told they are important.

This is not the future.

Not yet. No way. Shit, we may never see the future. How about that? When does *this* become *then*? The future is tangibly close and terribly far away. It is always happening, but it never actually happens.

No. This is later. Six months, give or take. Stephen and Neil are married now. It was a nice ceremony, but I felt sort of weird. That whole waiting-for-the-bride part. It seemed kinda weird to me, but whatever. They live in a beautiful rowhome down by the river and are thinking about adopting a Korean boy in a few years. I was sort of concerned they'd try to fuse their sperm together in a big bucket of joint-compound.

My mother is most likely addicted to pills. She says they're Percocets for the pain in her hip but it's probably MDMA or something. She is seeing Jerry a lot nowadays and there is some talk of her moving in with him but I don't think she'll leave her home. She's been doing a lot of charity work since my father died. That batch of brownies she baked all by herself? Regular good old non-organic flour. We're talking gluten.

Brian's still at the bookstore and still trying to nail college girls. There isn't senior liberal arts major he hasn't hit on. Really. He's planning on taking a month off to visit Europe. He's sure he's going to spend at least ten days in Amsterdam.

I still go to my shrink, but only once a week. I just don't have the time anymore.

Me, I'm sitting on my sofa in my office. It's a new leather sofa. I have all new office furniture since I have an all new office since I have an all new show. Me, I'm the talk show host for a one hour talk show on pay cable called *TalkShowX*. None of that Comedy Central bullshit here.

Kyle and my producers decided that it would be in everyone's best interest if we changed my name to something not associated with multiple homicides so the show's full title is *TalkShowX with John Sterling starring William Meridan*. Through the genius of committee thought, they wanted to distance themselves from the very tragedy that they were attempting to exploit.

Face it, this whole book, every horrid page, is total exploitation.

What's going on now is I'm getting a blowjob. The girl right here, on her knees between my legs, her lips wrapped around my manhood, tongue pulsing over my head, she was on my show today and I can't quite remember her name. Laura? Lauren? Lori? It has got to be an "L" name, I know that much for sure. Names aren't important quite yet. They don't become important until the future.

■ ■ ■

It turns out her name was Bernadette. There's a knocking at the door, and she finishes me off with Kyle standing dismissively in the doorway. He tells me we had ten minutes to be at the studio. He reminds me the studio is twenty minutes away. He wants to know if I've ever taken a math class.

I pop three Valium in my mouth and wash them down with Gatorade. I assure him everything is just fine. My eyes are confidence. He has no choice but believe what I say. Everyone believes me now. I tell parents that their children are playing violent video games and these games make them want to kill. Oh yes. I have experts and everyone believes an expert. This misguided belief then translates to buying power via ratings ratings ratings.

I want twelve year olds who smoke crack.

I want mothers who sleep with their daughter's boyfriends.

I need people to fall madly in love with their plumber.

I need a couple who weighs a combined fourteen hundred pounds.

I want a frogurt-loving grave digger who bathes in a kiddie pool to protest his father's fourth wife. Double points if she's a blood relative.

I want bad meets train wreck with meth.

I want and want and I need and need.

While we're in the limo, on our way to spend three hours setting up promos and ads for the next two weeks, I call my new girlfriend. Her name is Katherine Dempsey. She does the promotions for the show. I know what you're thinking, it's dumb to be involved with someone at work. Sometimes it's odd, but it's *so* fucking hot when your girl says "Oh baby, it feels like you're getting 23% of the 18-42 white male demographic in your time slot" while her legs are over your shoulders and she's tweaking your nipple.

She reminds me that I need to sound tough in these promos. John Sterling is a hard ass. John Sterling kicks ass and doesn't take shit. William Meridan couldn't do that, but John Sterling can.

I'm standing in the recording booth doing the voice-overs for the lead-in from Commercial.

Have you walked in on Daddy having sex with someone who's not your mommy? If so, please call...

Does your teacher worship Satan? If so, please call...

Does your lover mock your body odor? If so, please call...

If you've slept with the football team, and you'd do it again, please call...

If you think your sibling is too fat or ugly and shouldn't reproduce, please call...

On the next TalkShowX, *people with a fetish for dead rodents...*

On the next TalkShowX, *incest among same sex siblings...*

On the next TalkShowX, *fecalphiliacs and the spouses who love them...*

After I call out for the dumb and moronic of America to call me, it's time for make-up.

After make-up, production people are coming up to me, telling me the things I need to know for today's show. Who is going to do what, any special guests we might have, any special people in the audience, John cares about these things. Today's show- *Obese Teenagers and the Boyfriends Who Love Them*. Today a fight will break out. Today a girl's halter top will be accidentally removed. Today, I pander to the lowest common denominator. Today is like every day in the last six months.

I am told there are only ten minutes until the taping begins. I sit in my dressing room, deciding which amphetamine I am going to take. Do I want harsh and clinical or do I want warm and jovial?

Screw it, we can have both. I digest a handful of blue and peach colored pills. I don't remember the specific name, but they were fun yesterday. A mic is put into my hands. My tie is straightened. I am given a handful of index cards with all sorts of wonderful information on them.

Jennifer Mays: 17: 275 lbs: Tim Brown, bf: "She's a fat cow of a girl": calls her Jenny Craig in public.

They give me stacks of these cards. All I need to know about these people. Pertinent quotes. Life summaries. Amusing anecdotes. All typed neatly on a 3x5 card.

What I'm trying to say is people's lives are reducible to an index card.

A few bullet points. More like footnotes, really. That's what distinguishes these people.

The show begins and the first guest, Jennifer, is brought out and takes a seat stage right of me. Jennifer comes out and is seated. She tells her story, how kids used to make fun of her at school, parents who call her a pig and lock the fridge, a boy-friend who belittles her.

Trust me, no one could belittle Jennifer if you get what I'm trying to say.

"A boyfriend who belittles you?" begs the audience. "Can we meet him?" Of course they can. So can the home audience. I am an equal opportunity brain cancer. We bring out Tim. Everyone in the audience boos as he steps out on the stage and sits next to his girlfriend.

Me, I'm checking my hair off camera.

The boyfriend gives everyone the middle finger as he sits down. How wonderfully creative.

"Tim," I ask, "why do you say such mean things to your girlfriend? Do you love her?" Of course he loves her, he tells me, he'd "just love her more if she lost 60 pounds."

I'm not thinking Less Is More but I can't blame you if you were.

The audience keeps right on booing. Jennifer starts to cry. Tim gets defensive, saying fat little Jennifer doesn't do a thing to try and lose weight. She eats and eats and eats and never ever exercises. She used to weigh 155 pounds. and she sure looked sexy then, he assures us.

My mouth is getting dry. My fingers curl up like burning paper.

The way you feel when a friend is making a complete ass out of himself but you can't step up to shut them up, that's how I feel right now.

More crying fat women and more asshole boyfriends. Some have family or friends that are being supportive but the audience doesn't like them too much. One of the brothers gets into a fight with a boyfriend and then, what do you know, in the middle of the whole thing, a girl's shirt gets pulled off. Oops.

Due to careful planning, it was a slim sister, not a fat girlfriend.

The audience is on its feet, cheering and chanting, pumping fists and high-fiving. If I wasn't so medicated, this might bother me. Instead, I ask questions like:

Can you see your knees?

How many chickens do you eat in one day? How many can *you?*

Is it true you offered to cut open her thigh and vacuum out fat?

Being the caring nurturers that we are, we say that the winner of a wee little contest gets a two week all inclusive at a fat farm in San Diego! All they have to do is wear pig ears and, using only their faces, find three "truffles" in a wading pool full of chocolate pudding, run on all fours around the stage twice, squealing as loudly as possible, jump into a giant frying pan in the middle of the audience and "sizzle" for twenty seconds.

When we've taped enough, I tell the audience and viewers that obese people have feelings just like the rest of us and should be treated with respect and dignity.

■ ■ ■

It's that night and Katherine is working late, trying to get some radio attention for the show. On my way to my therapist's, Kyle calls me.

"Just wanted to let you know your latest residual check arrived. Five large isn't bad for doing nothing." That's a lot more usual. Most months it's under a grand. What gives?

"A big chunk is a payment from New Line Cinema. They want to use clips of the show in one of their upcoming movies. Made them show you the money *and* make it rain first."

"That's great," I tell him. "What's the movie about?"

"Didn't ask for a script, Will. I asked for a check. Cha-mother fucking-ching! Kapeesh?"

I'm about three minutes out from my therapist's so I ask if he has anything else for me.

"Just an idea I want you to think about. Diversification."

"I don't handle my investments personally," I explain to him. "I pay a guy to do that."

"Not what I'm talking about, Will the Pill. Not your money. Diversifying *you.*"

I don't know the difference between a 401(k) and a Roth so I really can't grasp what he's getting out here. Maybe a surgical procedure?

"Baby, you are more than a talk show host," he continues. "Don't get pigeon holed. Branch out. Diversify."

"You mean like going from a weatherman to a talk show host?"

"No, numb nuts, I mean rising above the sophomoric world of television."

"And how does that happen?"

"Well, I have an offer for you to play yourself in a cameo in a movie."

Diversify myself by playing myself?

"It will get you into a movie. From there, acting roles. Maybe pop up in the season finale of a TV show. Sky's the limit with you, baby."

I tell him I'll think about and hang up as I'm pulling into the therapist's parking lot.

I go in and there's no wait so I'm seated in less than a minute. He wants to know how I enjoy fame. Notoriety. I tell him it gets me up every morning and lays me down every night. It pays the bills, I say. It has its ups and downs. Highs and lows. Peaks and what do you call them? Valleys.

But I like the attention. I like the money. And with all the pills, sometimes I even like the show. But I don't mention the pills.

My head is a long vacant hallway. All fluorescent light and off-white walls and a vanishing point. You can hear electricity buzzing around you. Each outlet hisses.

For as wide as my eyes are, I can't really see a thing. Maybe my eyes aren't totally dilated, but it feels like my left eye can only focus really close, and my right eye can only focus on the distance. It's like sitting in a frozen car, trying to see through nine inches of ice on the windshield.

He asks if I still have dreams about my father. Not anymore, I tell him. What I don't tell him is I don't have dreams anymore. Sleeping is just down time. I stare at him for twenty seconds until I realize he probably asked me something different.

Nope, there's no newly found inner strength. There really isn't what's called faith, either. There is no drive, no ambition. There is never any relief. There is no mind set for success.

There are only new markets to carry my show. There are only new viewers. Dollar signs and percentage points.

He tells me I am distant now. He tells me I need to communicate. He says I was much more open before I became a talk show host, that I was making great strides towards progress. He tells me I'm regressing. I stare at him.

Blink, he goes away.

Blink, he's back again. Blink, blink. Blink, blink.

He asks about my relationship with Katherine. That's code for 'Are you ok about Monica?' I tell him I'm fine, we're fine. We've both been busy but we, you know, find the time. I don't mention all the women I've slept with over the last few weeks. It's got to be around 15 or so. Maybe more. It's hard to recall names when you can't even remember them as separate and distinct entities.

My relationship with Katherine is one of convenience. We are symbiotic, like the Great White and those stupid scavenger fish that follow them around. The only important question is:

Who's the shark and who's the scavenger?

Since I'm the one on TV and don't have semen running down my chin, it's easy to say I'm the shark. Like relationships are ever that easy. No, there's more going on.

Katherine is having an affair, but I have no clue with whom.

I'm screwing every white trash trailer park piece of waste that blows through the studio.

I am so totally dying to fuck Katherine's assistant but can't find a good in.

I can't dump Katherine because our relationship is sort of secret around work and she's the type who'd blab around the studio about me.

So I'm not exactly Jaws, if you get my point. What I am trying to say here is status means jackshit when everything gets broken down.

My therapist needs to know if I'm taking pills. Oh, I've had a few Prozacs, you know, here and there. Prozac, he tells me, is no little thing. Prozac, he says, is a dangerous drug that can easily lead to addiction. He tells me the first sign. He tells me the second sign. He even tells me the third.

But no, I show none of his signs. He has it all wrong anyway. The first sign of addiction isn't denial or rejection or projection or any of that. The first sign is oblivion.

Haven't been to work in a week? Pop a Lithium and have a stiff drink. No bowel movements for three days? You need a glass of warm milk and a Pamalar. Didn't realize you were taking over twenty pills a day? Oops.

Didn't realize there wasn't a safety net? Oops.

Didn't realize that you weren't the center of attention? Oops.

Suddenly you wake up in the middle of the night and realize that everything before had been a lie. You need to start all over. It's not like kindergarten taught you much different. Need to take a potty? Raise your hand.

Need to raise the hits on your website? Sell your soul.

It's all one and the same.

Consider my soul sold. I couldn't bounce a check for the life of me. I have six platinum cards.

My foreign revenue? Let's just say ninety grand a year, after taxes. I don't get Euro tastes, but they clearly get mine.

As long as I play the game, life is good.

21

When you are famous and you change your name, your family has some issues with the transition. My mother, who swore up and down she would never call me John, now only calls me John. Stephen, well he just calls me "bro" or "dude" most of the time. To them, I'm a different person.

To me, I am a different person.

Cher problems. Madonna concerns. The Edge's dilemma.

Today's show is *The Klu Klux Klan and Those They Have Hate Crimed.* A group of mentally challenged chimpanzees come out, dressed in ornate white robes, complete with matching hood and fancy red and black belts, proceed to tell me that the future of America is being challenged by these sub-human minorities. They are the ones ruining our schools. They are the ones who make the streets unsafe at night. They are the reason that white folks can't get a job.

Like their single digit IQ isn't a hindrance to gainful employment.

So we bring out some minorities. A black guy from Alabama, two black ladies from Tennessee, a Cuban from Miami, a few others, and they sit audience right on the stage. We have extra security tonight. We don't want race riots, just racial tension.

Audience members point out that God made us in His image, that we all are his children. An audience member asks one of the racists if he's proud of all the harassment he admits to giving to blacks in his home town.

"You're God damn right I am. I'm the only one of you white people strong enough to fight for our cause." I'd guess he's not talking about a charity, but one never knows anymore. The KKK Toddlers with Leukemia Drive. The KKK Walk for Literacy.

It's these shows, the ones with such rampant stupidity and ignorance playing up to all the hate, that actually bother me. Tomorrow's show won't bother me one bit: Autistic Children with Tourette's Syndrome.

One of the hate-mongers points out that every black rapper, "don't speak no good American." Good call, big guy.

I can feel the Zanax fighting with the Valium in my stomach. A stomach ache never felt better.

I can feel the heat of the zillion lights in the studio. I can hear the whirl of the recorder in the camera, recording all of this for posterity. Me, I'm running a hand through my hair to add a little body and scoping that sweet blonde with the dynamite rack in the fifth row.

I tell the audience, "Remember to love your neighbor, not hate their skin. Tomorrow on *TalkShowX*, autistic children with an affliction that further clouds their personal hell. Tomorrow, right here.."

And we're clear.

■ ■ ■

With all these shows that don't have teen sluts on them, a good three-way has been hard to find. The producer says you need to do more conservative shows over the holidays, the kids are home from school. Every sixth grader needs to see *I May Be Your Lover But I Slept With Your Brother.* It's strictly educational programming, I swear. I'm so doing this for the kids.

I ask the producer when we're going to be doing another cokehead stripper mom show. Five weeks. That's way too long from now. I need next week. I need tomorrow. I need yesterday.

It's not like I sleep much anymore. I may lie in bed for a few hours every night, but there's no rest. There's really no way to rest in a bed with Katherine.

I go home and spend sometime with her. We may eat dinner, a little talk about the show, upcoming promos, you know, foreplay. After that is the sex, the hot sweaty type where you have to peel off the sheets to go to bed and seriously rethink your ventilation scheme so you don't get black mold. This woman is a total and complete sex maniac. You knew she was in the mood when she would walk up behind you and whisper in your ear Make it rape, big boy. Most girls would say Faster or Deeper. She would say Make me bleed. Hurt me. Punish my evil. Fill me with cock.

She is amazing in bed but I have to wonder about her maternal skills.

We're talking about a woman who has burnt salads cooking. We're talking about a woman with a sixteen inch dildo named Vlad the Impaler. We're talking about a woman who slaps you if you come first.

And it's not like I want it to turn me on, but it does.

I'm not thinking Husbandry but I can't blame you if you were.

We talk briefly about plans to visit my mother next weekend. We still have four more days of shows to do. *Autistic Children with Tourette's Syndrome. Lovers Reveal Their Secret Fetishes. So What If I'm 12, I Wanna Sell My Body. I Assaulted My Pregnant Mother.*

I really need to focus here, buckle down and wrap this up. We're in negotiations with a media conglomerate which would carry us on their website, free for their customers. The network is behind it because of ad venues that are freaking huge. Three years, 4.2 million. And, as we all know, when you expand domestic coverage, you expand foreign threefold. Money making money, son.

I tell Katherine about my mother. She's a health nut, I say. She's an amazing passive aggressive. She is the alpha male of the family.

This is a woman who has exploded major holiday meals. She's embarrassed every family member a million times by now.

Katherine gets turned on by all of this and it's time for Round Two.

22

If you need to imagine autistic children with Tourette's Syndrome, what you want to think about is retarded midgets on crack. You probably don't need to.

I do feel bad for these kids but the ratings are incredible. People eat this sort of stuff up. People love seeing children in misery and the parents that love them.

Upon meeting Mark, the first thing out of his mouth is "cunt farts." Lovely. Good thing we have the handy dandy black box. The only other things he ever says are "dingus" and "Mark". He is twelve and his father tells us he has the intelligence of a four-year-old.

"Cunt farts."

His parent's tell us that someone played an Andrew Dice Clay tape somewhere as a joke and since then, well, it's about all the boy says. It's time for audience questions. It's time to scale the abyss.

"Hey, you know if my kid talked like *that*, I'd wash his mouth out with soap!"

"Well, sir, he hardly realizes he's being rude. He is only trying to communicate with us in the limited fashion he's able to."

"Dingus."

"Sir, he has no idea of right and wrong. He thinks like a toddler. Surely you don't punish a toddler for what comes out of their mouths."

"So, what's this kid, retarded or something?"

He has autism.

"So? My hands are killing me and I can still talk."

That's arthritis.

"So why's he keep yelling crap?"

That's Tourette's Syndrome. You uncontrollably say things.

"Yeah, well, if it was my kid…"

Applause. And we didn't have to flash the sign. I can feel the Darvocets kicking in and this all seems normal. Perfectly fine.

What you fail to understand, as a television viewer, is the timing and choreography that it takes to be a talk show host. It's all hit your mark hit your mark. Be here be there be here again. Not only do I need to find the right audience member for the quality question, an attractive girl has to be in the shot. You need to frame your shot that way. That's some tough stuff there.

There are still two more kids like Mark, but the audience likes him so much, the producer decides to run with just Mark out there. Makes him look rarer, more unique.

Like he's a collectible plate or something.

Wouldn't want to ruin the market for a semi-retarded child, now would you?

Mark's parents tell us how he doesn't even realize any of the potential dangers around him. If left unsupervised, he is liable to pick up a butcher's knife or run out into traffic.

And an audience member calls it survival of the fittest.

Mark's father and a guy wearing a Molson beer t-shirt get into a heated exchange about parental obligation. This is going nowhere quickly but when I gaze off camera at my director, he gives the stall signal. He wants me to sit back and let them go at it. Somewhere in Wichita, a divorced woman is eating this up.

If you want a lot of viewers, you need to find your demographic. Who do they want to watch? Then find those people, but in extreme situations. Like People Who Don't Masturbate or People Who Dated and Found Out They Were Related. There are millions of sexually repressed people, and everyone dates.

The show ends. Katherine wants me to do a record store grand opening. I say no. She insists. No way.

I have better things to do.

23

I never paid for sex until I had the money to buy the hot hookers. Why bother with the ugly ones, you can pick them up in bars. And the good looking ones, they usually are high class, can score a gram, and always provide the condom.

You might be thinking there's something wrong me because I like hookers. That I'm sexually perverted or I like to degrade women or something. Or maybe you're thinking because I can't get laid.

As if.

I just like the control. There's never any foreplay to worry about, and whether she comes or not isn't a concern. Hell, I'd be worried if she *did* cum.

They always ask, "So what do you feel like tonight/after breakfast/before the plane lands?" And you tell them.

Let's start off with some oral, a little around-the-world action and we'll finish with a Cuban Cannonball.

Maybe a Steamy Guatemalan. Every now and then, I'm a Diving For Pearls kind of guy. I'm always up for some Eiffel

Tower loving and I can never turn down a Reverse Jackhammer Irish style.

And I'll take a massage when we're done.

It's that easy.

Over time, you find the girls you really like. There's the cute blonde down on 7th and the hot redhead down on Walnut St. But if you're after anal, you need to speak with Beth down by the theater.

After you sleep with a hooker a few times, you open up a little. You tell your real name. Maybe your job, maybe your dog's name. Where you went to school, that sort of shit.

And she tells you shit, too. She won't ever tell you her real name, but her high school sweetheart? That's fair game. Her favorite teacher from elementary school? Yeah, Mr. Dawson.

It's not as much a relationship as it is a business transaction, where you know the cashier.

So that's how I got to be a regular for Amy.

She was a cute girl, with amazing legs that I picked up outside a club a few weeks ago. She had real spunk, a true go-getter. Once turned to twice turned to weekly turned to every damn day.

She doesn't care about Katherine, but she would be devastated if I ever slept with another whore. Unless, you know, I want anal with Beth.

Amy doesn't do anal. Not even with a regular.

24

Today is another day where the Earth wasn't destroyed by a meteor the size of Texas crashing into a rice field in Asia so of course today's topic is Nymphomaniac Senior Citizens Who Discovered They Were Homosexuals In Nursing Homes.

This is an underserved demographic, I swear.

Our first guest is Ron. Ron is 73, lost a ring finger in Nam, has 4 grandchildren, and loves to "smoke thick pole".

I'm checking his two cards to see if this guy is for real or a paid actor but I can't tell. Real or fake, it's all the same. My tie is outstanding today.

So Ron, I ask, how did this turn of events happen?

"My best guess is pussy fatigue."

I going to need more that vaginal weariness.

"So it's like this- there's only so much you can do with a pussy. You can only nail it dick-first."

This guy has never met my promotion head. She's probably off stage, taking this as a personal challenge right now. I should be getting aroused but I'm talking to a 73 year old man.

Ok, good point though. But when?

"Probably when the sponge bathes didn't work."

Didn't... work? This is a Valium segment. Why did I go with Lorazepam? Someone is getting fired. I need two shots of whisky lined up quickly, off stage. One, smokey with a strong peat aftertaste, and the other with that straight gasoline burn. And, of course, a Valium. I make the needed hand signals and carry on, ever the consummate professional.

"Yeah, didn't work. You know, they give you that sponge bath. They rub the nipples. They work the inner though. They tease the balls. But the tease didn't go nowhere any more."

Ok, that's a good start to get the audience worked up so they can do a crowd pan shot and I can knock those shots back, but mostly, they are disgusted. Sigh. I need the crowd to get next level grossed out but they are still seeing Ken as a grandfather figure. Again- a Valium segment.

"Well, you ever jack your dick and think to yourself *I can do this better than a woman can?*"

No, but yeah.

"Well, extrapolate that to blowjobs."

You can blow yourself better? Interesting but not really in the narrative here. And disgusting on fifteen levels. And I'm realizing that a man who collects Social Security is discussing jerking off and blowjobs with my nationwide audience and I'm not finding this that *that* strange.

"It's like, look, you can't blow yourself..."

-Wrong, that show is in three weeks-

"...but you already know what's what. You have the skills, the knowledge, the understanding. The power."

This garners groans from the crowd, but they are still in the 'uhhh, this is a grandpa' stage and not giving me enough time to knock back those shots. They are lined up.

They are sitting there. I have good staff.

I need a second here. Not because gramps sucks cock or anything, but I really want those shots and they have them lined up and right now, they are playing with my emotions. So I do the 'remove the glasses' into the 'eye squint' into the 'fist on chin'. Hopefully, camera two was on point and zoomed in during the eye squint.

I'm not thinking Blue Steel but I can't blame you if you were.

I'm trying to wrap my head around this. Part of this makes perfect sense to me. The rest of me is nauseated.

So you had an interest in orally pleasuring another man? Experimentation? OK, that's a normal thing.

"So I blew four guys at once. Circus seal-style."

All of me is nauseated.

Right. Nymphos. I forgot.

I'm not thinking Greatest Generation but I can't blame you if you were.

It's not like I'm a homophobe. I don't care what consenting adults do. But this guy is collecting Social Security checks and heading to a lemon party. My Jacob and Co. cufflinks can't overcome that.

And the audience is gone. This is ageism times homophobia times my sweet grandfather so I am getting my cheek makeup reapplied while those shots disappear.

Shot shot shot. Gone.

I would have preferred to not have ended on the gasoline, but they are redoing my hair so I'm fine.

Usually, the audience loves my gay guests. Teens kicked out of their parent's house because they were gay. Gay fathers. Man-on-man cousinly love. My audience is way into transgendered people. But they are not liking this.

This is what it takes to put them outside of their comfort zone.

■ ■ ■

I haven't smoked a cigarette in over a month now. I just realized that. I guess I can stop cold turkey without even trying to. Will power?

Not even.

I just don't have time for those things. If I can't get messed up either quickly or while I work, then I just don't need to get messed up.

I also haven't had more than three or four drinks. I've only gotten high on pot once since *TalkShowX* started, and that was just a quick bowl with the main speaker of an anti-drug show. Since he's a professional athlete, I'm not going to name names, but let's just say he's rushed for over a thousand yards more than once.

It's amazing how much time goes into this show. You need to have people prep the guests. You need someone to hand out questions for the audience to ask. You need other people to script this all out. You need a team of lawyers to acquire the rights to the name "TalkShowX" because some god damned

Australian public access show already uses it. You need people to find guests and to come up with relevant topics.

Not everything is relevant. Off the top of my head, I can think of at least a dozen shows that didn't meet our high standards of excellence. *Virgins Who Were Raped And Became Nymphomaniacs. Ex Child Pornography Stars. I Can Only Have Group Sex.*

I Sold My Child For Narcotics. Criminally Insane Who Wish To Adopt. The Prose And Poetry Of Convicted Murderers.

My Pet Looks Like A Sex Organ.

Men Who Can Self Fellate.

Trisexuals. The Four Thousand Pound Couple. Johnnie Depp Groupies. Schizophrenic Albino Lesbians Midgets. I'm Addicted To S & M.

God Cured My Gay.

Sometimes good taste wins out, if you can call this good taste. If triggering a full-body gag reflex can be considered taste period.

You need other people to sell your show to new areas. You need mules. Grinders. Low wage, dirty mother fuckers that do the heavy lifting. You need people to do the hard work, be the servants and whatnot. You need people behind the scenes. You need people to run the cameras and lights. You need people to edit.

At the end of the day, that infrastructure stands invisible behind me. I am what you want. I have sophistication and elegance that subtly wins you over.

I've got more youtube subscribers to my clips than any other late night show, and it's election season, when the Colberts and Samantha Bees out there shine.

That's what this is all about. Competition on the open market. The circle of life. The little guy snapping up crumbs from the big table, nipping at the giants, chopping up Goliath. Can't you just smell the capitalism?

■ ■ ■

Today's show is *So What If I'm 12, I Wanna Sell My Body*. Already on stage is Maria, who has slept with over 20 men and has earned a steady income from sexual favors since she was 11, and Lisa, who has stripped for her sixth grade class to drive up sales. Their words, not mine.

Somehow, I'm doubt these girls have seen much *Sesame Street*.

As we bring out the next little tramp, Lindsey, the mood is Cro-Magnon. The girls insist they have the right to sell their body, after all, it is theirs, now isn't it? Sadly, I have this odd feeling that there are more than a few men in the audience who want to sleep with Lindsey. For twelve, she has large breasts. One of the producers told me that she was "stacked like IHOP", and as bizarre as it sounds, she is.

Her index card just says "titties for days".

The audience is applauding because we just brought out Sgt. Shock. He's an ex-Marine who comes on the show periodically as an intimidating presence. He likes to scream and the kids respond fantastically to it by curling up in the fetal position, crying and turning absolutely white.

I guess I should have added *Albino* to the show title.

Anyway, after he breaks down their walls, shrinks their self-worth, and tells the douche bags in the audience that he's

going to break their dicks off, he will show these kids the er-
rors of their ways. He's going to take them to a women's prison
and to a free clinic. He wants to show them what happens to
prostitutes and criminals. The audience just wants to see the
female inmates.

"So you want to strip for little boys, get their peters all
hard? You like that, huh? Well, girlie-girls, I have a whole new
world for you."

I had my teeth bleached yesterday so my smile is so bright
and radiant that the reflection off my teeth could be used to
combat cancer.

"You wanna strip? You wanna take your clothes off?
News flash, honey. They'll strip search you in prison. They'll
hose you down with cold water. They'll let other women violate you. They'll rape you. They'll beat you. No one will care.
You'll just be a God damn prisoner. Who gives a fuck about
prisoners?"

I'm not thinking Foot Long Double Dong but I can't
blame you if you were.

"Laugh and smile all you want, trash cunts, 'cause when we
get to lock down, someone else will be smiling ear to ear. Yes
indeedy." The girls are lead off stage, like cattle to the kill. Cut
to commercial.

Trash cunts? That's bold, even for Shock.

And we're back. The girls are walking down a prison corridor, and the inmates are catcalling the young girls.

"Tight pink, tight pink, tight pink, tight pink." In some
primitive way, I find this unsettlingly arousing. "Beav-er,
beav-er." It's all I can do not to think about chick prison flicks.

This vaguely lesbian ordeal goes on for three more minutes. Next, we're at the free clinic, where the girls are given photographs of sex organs ravaged from venereal disease.

This is a vagina oozing fluorescent yellow pus due to advanced gonorrhea.

This is a penis, purple, swollen and covered with blisters thanks to chlamydia.

This is a clitoris, bloody and sagging, with boils on it due to the effects of syphilis.

This is disease. This is rape. This is future, the end result. This is you.

I'm not thinking Foreplay but I can't blame you if you were.

Next, they meet some AIDS patients, whose faces are blurred over. They tell their stories. How they had to prostitute themselves for money. A 19 year old girl who was raped and contracted the virus. A 17 year old boy who ran away from home and ended up a male prostitute, orally pleasuring men for $25 a pop. Surprisingly, he was one of those sex-savvy types who used a fresh condom every time a man ponied up $75 for anal sex. Guess what? He still got AIDS.

Suddenly, we're back, live in the studio. The magic of editing. The girls are crying tears of joy and clutching their mothers. They all swear they'll behave and respect their bodies. The mothers are crying as well, telling anyone in earshot how much they love their daughters.

Of the five mother-daughter combos on stage, only one is actually related. The other four never met until the taping. They are actors, making $75.45 a day filming for talk shows, infomercials, maybe some soft core porn. It's not our standard practice to hire actors for the show, but there have been a few law suits filed about exploitation of minors. Until our lawyers straighten it all out, we'll continue to hire actors. Besides, it's getting harder and harder to get parents to sell their kids down the river on national television.

I'm not thinking Mothers Against Immoral Media but I can't blame you if you were.

After the taping, I have tantric sex for the first time with one of the mother-actresses after snorting an eighth of Bolivian flake from her more than ample chest. They say tantric sex can last for hours. It may have been those tantric exercises, but when I'm all coked up, it takes me forever anyway. And they say the orgasm builds up for hours so when you come it feels like an explosion, but when I tossed my wad, it was weaker than taking a leak after drinking a six pack.

Well, at least she was flexible.

25

If you're taking a lot of different pills, your urine changes color a lot. Now that I'm big on Vicodans and Valiums, my piss has a distinct blue tint, plus a deep musky odor. My eyes were starting to yellow, but my makeup lady gave me these drops that work wonders.

Another perk about fame is that you don't need to shave. Every Monday I have a full facial wax. No more razor burn, no more nicks on my Adam's apple. My face is as smooth as a baby's ass and I'm loving every minute of it.

Though I have excellent vision, the show has me wearing these high fashion frames with plastic lenses. They tell me it leads for greater facial expression.

Want disbelief? Look over the top of the lenses and down your nose.

Want interest? Take off the glasses and gaze intently.

Want pensive thought? Take them off, squint, and nonchalantly chew the arm.

I'm the Rick Perry of late night pay cable talk shows.

Sometimes they like me to wear suits with a vest. They swear it makes me more likable. People have to want to see me. The show's topic, that's unimportant. They watch me. I am the product. I'm the whore and the production company is my pimp.

Pimp me, whore me, pay me.

Film me, edit me, pay me.

Yeah, it really is this easy.

Wear earth tones, pause in the middle of sentences to feign thought, never smile too big.

For the last *Cokehead Stripper Moms* show, they gave me these little orange pills to keep me from getting a hard on during the show, as the mothers would be stripping for us, you know, with their kids there. How stimulating! Anyway, me popping wood on national television wouldn't endear me to middle America. They put this powder stuff in my hair so it doesn't get reflective.

Nowadays, I can't stroll down MLK Boulevard looking for cocaine and or uppers. I just send an aide. I'm what they call a role model, so I can't get caught during the solicitation of a hooker.

I have a fan club on every continent except Antarctica. Screw the Beatles, I'm bigger than Jesus.

My contract states that I have to go to six charity functions a year. The show gives me the money to donate. I already have two down in two months, the Ugandan Christian Missionary Network and a breast cancer dinner in New York. Since a PBS fundraiser counts, I'm doing one in Pittsburgh, if we can break through in the marketplace. They want me to show up, yinz better tune in.

And for those people not from Pittsburgh, "yinz" is the dumb way of saying "y'all" which is also dumb. Whatever.

■ ■ ■

It is a Friday taping, so that means an intervention. Today it is a man addicted to pornography. Last week, some *Shopoholics*. Next week, *Video Game Junkies*.

Dave's family comes out, all sad that Dad seems more interested in porn than them. If that was my wife and kids, I'd be spending more time "reading the articles", too.

These shows don't require much from me, I just sit back and watch it happen. Occasionally, I have to say something like "But Dave, can't you see your wife is in pain?" or "How can you do this do your family?" Other than that, we're talking cruise control here. Hell, I don't even prep for these shows anymore.

Afterwards, I'm looking for Katherine. About work or about sex, I don't know yet. I could use some head, but there's always work related shit she wants to talk about.

It's not that I mind the work or anything, but sex is so much better. Those people who get gratification through their work? Those people are fucking idiots.

No one's seen Katherine. No one in Promotion. No one in Production. No one in Editing. She's gone, vanished, disappeared. Usually she's so far up my ass, she's stepping on my prostate. But not today.

Normally, if I can get rid of Katherine for a few hours, I call up Amy and have a "date". But Amy's in Toronto for a week visiting her sick father. Who knew hookers had families?

I'm looking up and down for my girlfriend. Studio One? Nope. Studio Two maybe? Wrong.

She's not in a meeting and I know she's here today, I saw her car in the parking lot.

I open the door to the camera storage room. That's where I found Katherine.

Being fucked by a camera guy.

He has her bent over a camera and keeps saying "What now, bitch? What now?"

I clear my throat. "Oh, so sorry to interrupt here."

"Man, John." The dude is breathing hard. "You want in on this?" Katherine is just staring at me.

"Um, no, Mike. See, that's my girlfriend. I'm already in on that." They're not even stopping.

"Really? I'm fucking John Sterling's girlfriend? Oh man." Then he makes that grunt all guys make when they come, pulls out, and tosses all over the camera.

"What the hell are you doing?"

"Busting a nut, man. Duh."

"Not you, Mike, her."

Katherine, pulling her panties up and adjusting her skirt, looks at me. "Don't even start, John. I know you're laying more pipe around here than a god damn plumber. Every slut on the show, you're sticking her. Every one."

"So you fuck a camera guy?"

"And that Amy. Don't give me that 'she's a massage thera-pist'. Bullshit, John, bullshit."

"Whatever, Katherine. Well, I guess it's over. And, you're fired. Ship your ass back to public access. And, Mike, you too. Later, folks." Out of sight, out of mind. This never happened.

"You can't fire me, I'm union."

Did I stutter or something? "Mike, you're fired. Your break ended ten minutes ago, and you blew your load on a $115,000 camera. Oh, let's add sexual harassment for asking me to join in. Buh-bye."

They're both protesting but I turn and walk away. It's one thing for me to cheat, but at least I'm not cheating with a fuck-ing camera man. I have standards.

Ok, not standards, more like... well...ok, I fuck pretty much everything. But not in a storage room. And not with an over weight camera man. And I don't get caught.

What I want to know here is why do all the women in my life feel this need to express themselves sexually all over the place. If it's not on film, then it's at least on a camera. What is it with our society? Back in the day, women repressed their sexu-ality. They were called names if they enjoyed sex. Shunned. Burned at the stake. Now? They don't just enjoy it, they get first dibs on that enjoyment. Girl's Night. They drink for free, they get in for free. Equality my ass.

It's not as much sex any more as it is a political statement.

By taking it in the ass, they're saying, it's my ass and I like it like this.

A fuck is as much a vote as it is a way to populate the world.

I'm not thinking Rock The Vote but I can't blame you if you were.

As disgusted as I am right now, I need some pills in a big way. I'm thinking 800 mgs of Percoset, a few lines of coke, perhaps a Vicodan later, if that all settled.

26

So now I'm out an assistant. Not just any assistant, but my promo assistant. The most important one. That's the one that schedules everything and ensures I follow through on all of it. Pretty much my *personal* assistant.

I have to hire someone. I can't *not* have a promo assistant. Who's going to sign the paperwork for me? Who's going to stall some random guy while I rail his wife or sister or daughter or whatever? Who's going to get my drugs?

WHO is going to get MY drugs?

I decided to call Brian and ask him if he was interested.

"You want a job?"

Pause. "Huh?"

"A job. You know, career."

"Dude, I own my own business. The bookstore, remember?"

"Yeah. But seriously man. I mean something like the promotion head for my show."

"Are you on a bad trip? A bookstore, dude. I own one.?"

"Ok, I'll play along. I'll play along because I like you, Brian. Because you still may be high from Amsterdam shrooms. I'll ask. So, what eighteen year old British lit major are you trying to fingerfuck? Does she have a nice rack? Did you get her by quoting a Bronte sister? Charlotte, of course. Does she have a hottie roommate for me? Please, oh please say she does."

"Fuck you, dude. What's your point?"

"My point is I'm offering you a job in show business and you're still worrying about statutory rape laws."

"You know, you are such a prick now that you're on TV. For a star, you sort of suck."

"Whoa killer. Let's not go saying things we can't take back."

"Besides, doesn't Katherine do that."

"She did. She's gone now. Creative differences. So, want the job?"

"Dude, I'm going to pass on that. Thanks anyway."

"Fine. Then any ideas on who I should hire? Any emerging faces come to mind?"

"What in the world are you talking about? Are you on coke again?"

"Coke? Ha, that's funny. *Coke.* Right. No way, man. So, want to have a drink this evening? Skibble's at seven." He'll see me there, he says.

■ ■ ■

Sunday I had to look over paperwork. Various contracts, proposals, and outlines have been around for my perusal and peruse them I have not. There was a proposal for a movie based on the show, but also a spin-off tv show about the security guys.

There's the outline on a book of dirty jokes "written" by me. A fucking outline.

Section one, Women.

Q: What's the difference between spit and swallow?

A: Forty pounds of pressure on the back of her head.

Can you get a Pulitzer for dirty jokes?

There's a proposal for a 3 DVD set of "uncensored, hardcore antics by the most out of control people yet!!!" that will make me a mint. The problem is that it's a steaming pile of shit. The only nudity happens in a fight between two overweight strippers and in all of the fight scenes, there's at most, four punches that land. Besides that, there's only the novelty of actually hearing the curse words.

I worry sometimes about the over exposure. If you hype something enough, eventually someone will make fun of it. There is always backlash. Kyle swears I am miles from overexposure but I'm not quite sure anymore.

We just spent almost two million dollars on highway billboards and three hundred thousand on television, plus we usually get four minutes a day free because we have a show on the network. My face is on the side of, like, half the fucking buses around here.

I'm not going to sign any of this stuff yet, it can all wait one more day. I have a meeting with Kyle in the morning anyway. No need to rush this. By tomorrow I'll have someone working for me. I need to have someone to buy my pills and arrange my sex. I am a busy man and I have complicated needs and I can not waste a second of my valuable time. I make $12 a second, showtime. One dealer works in the muscle relaxers, another for the coke and yet another for the uppers and downers. Not to mention the back-ups for when the primaries go dry or run hot. And besides all of that, there is the actual business of all the talk show itself, the contracts and planning and whatnot.

I can't even read this crap anymore. The words are all blurring together and all this fine print is retarded.

I take three Paxil and go to bed. Funny thing about Paxil. I can *never ever* get off if I take it. It makes being in front of an audience and cameras a lot easier, but let's face it- the sex is more important.

■ ■ ■

The next morning, Kyle comes into my office without even knocking and drops a box of bagels on my desk. They're all pre-sliced with two tubes of low fat cream cheese. "Good morning, sunshine," he sing-songs to me. I hate morning people.

"Morning, Kyle. Look, I was going over those product offers and I'm not sure. A branded joke book? That just seems bizarre. I mean, the DVDs are probably a good call but…"

"Stop right there," he says holding up his hands. "Those are small potatoes. And speaking of potatoes, have I got a great offer that just came in for you."

"If it's for my own personal line of artisan potatoes, I swear I will beat you senseless."

"Close but no, baby. We're talking a boxed meal delivery program." His eyes are wide and gleaming so either there's good money to be had, or he is totally fucking with me. Since I can't tell, I just stare blankly until he continues. "They mail out these boxes with pre-made meals in them. Some of them even have done some prep work. Either way, these people feel like a French fucking chef."

"Kyle, I'm as culinary as a McDonald's drive thru. This makes no sense."

"It's not about sense, baby. It's about projecting an image."

"What fucking image are we projecting? Who is the target here? I doubt people who buy uncensored DVDs are buying meal boxes delivered to their homes."

"There's plenty of overlap. This is where we branch you out a bit. First, there's two categories. "Homestyle", which targets the current *TalkShowX* demographic. Market it as stuff your mom makes. We're talking meatloaf, sloppy joes, basic shit. Next, "Entrepreneur" which is obviously more upscale and is aimed at the crowd who has more money and may not watch your show as much, but knows who you are and why you are famous."

"I'm famous because some deranged cat lady shot up her wedding reception."

"Not to these people. You, baby, are a talk show rock star."

"A rock star has nothing to do with food," I counter. He is unfazed.

"Look, even Tom Brady has a program. What's he got to do with food?"

"I'm pretty sure he's well known for having a strict diet, you know, like lots of professional athletes. I can see marketing his diet. I don't have a diet."

"They'll give you a diet. They said you can have input into the meals."

"I don't want input, this is stupid."

Kyle is openly exasperated with me. I'm guessing either they offered him a signing bonus to get me on board or a year of free meals.

"Baby, you need to branch out. Expand your brand. Claim new territory."

As much as he has point about expanding my name recognition, I feel like this new territory is akin to claiming northern Greenland. Why?

"And if this thing works out, there's tons of follow-on opportunities. Infomercials. That type of stuff."

I get this nauseating feeling the end state is hawking reverse mortgages during soap operas.

"Look, Kyle, this just doesn't seem right to me, at least for right now. I'm not going to go with it."

"There's a twenty thousand dollar signing bonus for you and 3% of all meal sales."

Every man has his price.

In.

27

I knew that I couldn't hire another woman for the job. Chances are, I'd just rail her like everyone else, and therefore have the same dilemmas. So a guy, then. A guy who would have to be a complete and total freak with, at best, a loose grip on reality, yet still relatively highly functioning. The answer was simple.

Josh.

Early Tuesday morning I sent Josh an email stating that I'd love to meet with him to discuss a business opportunity. I included directions to my office and 'Thanks, see you at noon.'"

Josh showed up ten minutes early. My lovely secretary led him into my office and got two cups of coffee. Josh sat and nervously stuffed his hands into his pockets to keep from fidgeting as he stared off into the corner while I added milk and sugar to my cup.

"So, how are things down at the station?"

"You know, pretty much the same. They are going to start giving the guys in R&D flex time, so that'll be nice."

"Cool. And the rapping thing? That working out?"

"Um, no, never really happened. Now I'm trying to start a goth band and call it *Voltaire's Grave*. Wear black, whine a lot, you know. Anyway, your email said something about a business opportunity."

Of course it did. It's about a job... no, a *career* in show business.

Doing what, Josh asks me.

"Oh, fair enough question. You'd be my promotions and acquisitions manager. You'd be in charge of, well, promotions. Of many, many types. Sometimes you have to be the right person for the crowd. Sometimes it's negotiating over radio promo time. Sometimes you'll need to go and pick me up condoms. Really, everyday it's something different. You'd pretty much be my assistant. And let me tell you, there are plenty of side perks, if you get my flow." Wink, wink, nudge, nudge, know-what-I-mean, know-what-I-mean.

"Uh-no."

"Hot sex, Josh, plenty of hot steamy sex. Pretty much all of the time."

"Really?" Yes, Virginia, there is a Santa Claus and his stage name is Casual Sex.

"Yeah, man. Come on, you'll be working with people who appear on a fucking talk show after all. They're not God damned Mensa members or anything. Think about it. If she's dumb enough to show up and talk about how she likes sucking guys off on *national* television, yeah, she'll blow you after the show. This is not, like, trigonometry or some shit."

"Is that legal?"

Legal? Well, you don't pay them and they consent. Is that legal?

"How much do I make?"

Eighteen hundred a week green, five hundred in white.

"Huh?"

Oh, how I miss such sweet naivety.

"Green is cash, white is coke."

"But I don't do coke."

"This is show business; you'll learn to do coke. It's no biggie, you'll get two weeks paid detox each year."

"So, ok, when do I start?"

"Right now. Today, you'll spend the day with Ryan. He's in Operations. Tomorrow, you'll be with Anthony. He does Production. Then, on Friday, you're in the big show with me. By next week, you should be able to do 90% of your job, no problem."

With that, Josh joined the *TalkShowX* team, and we started on the path that ends in a six state manhunt, utilizing over two hundred law enforcement officers.

28

By Thursday, Josh had acclimated himself well to the set. He was now assertive, which is good as it made people respect him. He gave a command and it was usually followed quickly. By Friday, he was doing lines at every break and referred to the guys in make-up and wardrobe as his "little faggots."

I think he was screwing Becky, the set manager and I know he got a blow job from a guest from Wednesday's show, You're Too Fat To Go And Wear That. Apparently, Josh was a chubby-chaser, though he just said he liked his women built for speed.

Movement or the drug, I had no fucking idea.

By the start of his second week, Josh was unstoppable. He weeded out unwanted calls, he always had a bump or two for me if needed, and took absolutely zero bullshit from anyone. If a cameraman was late getting back from break, Josh was liable to in his face, lips to ears hissing a gentle reminder that while fucking off *can* be fun, Sgt. Shock will break it off if you're late again. He also took to putting trace amounts of speed in guest's water, just to give them "that edge."

Sure, I could no longer fuck my assistant, but Josh came up with the great idea of secretly taping our little sexual indiscretions. It's not just posterity, he tells me. It's like hanging the head of an elk over your fireplace after you hunted it across whatever African country gave you a hunting permit. It's why you frame diplomas, or make space on your bookshelf for some knick knack from a small Asian country no one has heard of. It's all trophy fucking, at the end of the day.

"Besides," he says in a quiet tone, "it's an homage to Monica. When you are sticking it to them, you're sticking it to her."

And they say good help is hard to find.

The man also always had a condom for me. Talk about clutch.

Not only has Josh been a Godsend for my sex life, he had some creative ideas for the show as well. He came up with an idea for a closing segment where I sermonize about the evil of the day's show and spout a few words of wisdom. The name of the segment- hold it for a second- "Sterling Moments." Now that's beautiful.

Albino Lesbian Midgets- "It is a sad day when someone is targeted with hateful slurs and blatant discrimination just because they lack skin pigmentation, height, and a normal sexual appetite. What is more important is their soul, their essence, their commitment to a better world, for us, and for them. Please, don't look down on these albino midgets."

Parents With Psychosis- "When did it become a bad thing to love your children? When did it become a crime to try and help the fruit of your loins to a place in a life better than your own? Just because someone suffers, and I mean suffers, from a debilitating mental disease that makes them unstable and unpredictable does not mean that they are unfit parents. Please, open your hearts and minds to the mentally challenged parents of America."

Seventeen-Year-Old Crack Whores- "It seems to me that we are blaming the wrong people here. Is it their fault that they have sex for crack, in a world that forces them to please men so the can feed the habit forced upon them by a system which ignores them and defeats any idea of a better life or decent health care? Who is the victim here? Please, look at both sides of an issue before chastising the crack whores of the world."

I feel much better knowing that I don't write this garbage. They tell me that every last sentence HAS to begin with "please" because it adds to the suggestive nature of my sermon. Am I the only one scared by the fact that people believe what I am saying? They think I'm sincere about this. They think I care. They think I'm a humanitarian. I think I need a few milligrams of Paxil and check with Josh to see where that wet, sloppy blow job is.

■ ■ ■

I'm in my office on the phone with my dear mother, so it's a Fentanyl afternoon. The only question is how many. I gotta find a stronger dosage of these lollipops. I tried two at a time once and got self-conscious that I looked like a fucking squirrel. I will put Josh right on that.

She's asking when I am going to visit again? Soon. Join her on a family vacation, maybe Europe? I'm due a production break in August, I tell her but there's no way I'm visiting Europe with mom. She reminds me I'm her only hope for grandchild so now it's also a Halcion afternoon as well. I just don't have time to find a woman, I tell her.

I'm too busy to date, I tell her.

Right now, I'm in career-mode so I will have enough time and money to do the family-mode thing the right way later, I tell her.

I'm burned out by nailing half of my guests that the thought of actively seeking sex seems very foreign to me, I don't tell her.

Today is an open episode, which means nothing is hard scheduled. This is where we usually bring people on who didn't make the time frame earlier in the week. People who were cut due to *Cranial Fetishes About Lice* or *People Who Mainline Toothpaste*.

Some episodes go long. You never know when *Nazi Sympathizers With STDs* are also trained bassoonist. These things happen. You can't walk away from a Nazi bassoon solo.

Try to. You can't.

I hear the audience getting loud and the voice guy doing the pre-show monologue so I know I'm less than 30 seconds out. Josh hands me the cards for the first guest and he's doing that looking away-biting his bottom lip thing that tells me we are about to either film a 217 week abortion, or the guest is totally hot and down with anal. I just don't know.

This is flip of the coin territory. Either/or.

As in *either* the Halcion is enough *or* Clozaril is needed as well.

So there I am, on stage, and there's applause and my tie clip is especially banging considering it cost less than $500. Josh isn't standing by on the stage right wing, so it's pretty clear we are in abortion territory. Fine. Whatever.

This teen girl, maybe 15 or or 16, walks out with her mother. They both look normal, not hooked on methamphetamines, and probably aren't down for a gangbang. They take a seat as I look at the first card and all it says is "Jessica / 16 / ask about her teeth".

That's the talk show equivalent of leading a witness.

Ok, fine.

"So, Jessica, welcome to the show. We're glad you could make it. My producer is telling me you have something interesting regarding your teeth."

"My *lack* of teeth."

Ahh, back to a teen meth episode. Nice. Been while.

But she seems happy about this. Most of these tweeters are at least embarrassed their face looks like the broken window of an abandoned home.

Can you tell us about your lack of teeth?

"First thing they ought to know", the mother interrupts, "is that this nonsense was *not* approved by me."

The audience is starting a low boo. Are they booing the mother's lack of parental control or the child's actions without parental permission? I don't know, but these are the questions that don't keep me up at night.

Before I can mull this dilemma further, the daughter starts calling her mom a possessive bitch and out to ruin her life. Same old, same old. If this crap is scripted, we need new writers.

"Hold on, hold on, hold on, ladies. Settle down. There's no need to call names." Some assclown in the back yells "fight fight" but that's going nowhere and the guy shuts up before security even moves towards him. My reflection in my Italian loafers is immaculate. Pristine. Hair *and* shoes.

They calm down a bit and Jessica is rolling her eyes but I still can't figure out what's going on here. Josh isn't off camera anywhere.

"Alright ladies, what's the story here, with missing teeth?" Direct. To the point. Frustrated and losing my buzz.

"This cum-bag has-"

"I've only slept with six guys, mom!"

"-has decided that getting rid of her teeth is some artistic statement."

What.

The.

Actual.

Fuck?

Jessica is going on with it's her body and her decision and it's empowering and now that I know what's going on, I'm more confused.

"Jessica, what is your mother talking about?"

So, the thing is, tattoos and piercings are lame now. Getting those thick gauge ear rings? Meh, that's straight wanna-be. But having teeth removed- functional, non-diseased teeth- is a bold statement of body art.

Having her left lower incisor removes shows solidarity with feminist causes.

Getting rid of one upper molar is to identify as gay, two as bi, and four as transgendered.

This is a thing.

She tells us this is empowering. She's in control of her body.

And the audience is enraged.

"Why would ya mess up a perfectly good mouth when I spend four grand on braces for my kid?!"

"You spent actual money to look like a meth whore?" I'm glad to see people jump to the same conclusions as me.

So Jessica says they don't understand, which is probably true about this and algebra, and her mom keeps trying to claim that the audience being on her side is proof she's right, which is a logical fallacy unto itself.

Suddenly, there's Josh, offstage, giving me the 'go to commercial' gesture so I say those words that lead to a commercial break and head back to get water and some pharmaceutical help for this, and as I walk by Josh, he whispers "dibs on the daughter."

29

I walk into my office on a, I guess, Wednesday, and there's Kyle and Josh sitting on my sofa like they live here. Before I can ever ask if they need amount alone, Kyle says, "You just got the big call, baby."

I feel like I'm supposed to know what this means but I haven't the foggiest.

"Huh?" I ask.

"The man called. He wants to speak with you. In person."

"Josh, translate."

"The chairman of broadcasting called from the network. He wants to meet you! Now!" Josh is smiling and squirming like a kid about to piss his pants.

"Take a seat, Will, baby," Kyle offers. "I'll walk you through this."

I remain standing, arms crossed.

"Anyway," he continues, "I was over at their main office this morning, delivering a pitch for some shitty comedy a client wrote. Straight jerk off material but whatever. So after he tossed the script in the shredder and told my client to get the fuck out, he asked about you."

My mind starts racing. Wait, this happened this morning? Their office is across town. There's no way. Then I check my cell and it's 11:23 and the story is completely plausible.

"What did he want to know?" I ask carefully.

"Your story, baby. What made you *you*. If you were legit real deal or just a flash in the pan."

"And?"

"And he wants to meet you. Right now. Time to get you into a limo, baby."

Five minutes later, I'm in the back of a studio limo with Kyle who is trying to talk me out of pills but you can't build a pipe bomb and then get all pissed when it goes off. I pop a few boring muscle relaxers, trying to show Kyle I'm taking this seriously.

The drive is decent for the lunch hour. I can't tell if I am nervous about this or irritated. On one hand, the Broadcast Chairman is like my boss's boss's boss and can crush me in a second. On the other hand, we still have taping to do and I have a pre-dinner anal engagement with Beth penciled in.

What I'm saying is I've got better things to do.

Correction. I shouldn't objectify women. I've got better whores to do.

We get there and take a private elevator up to the thirty-something floor but I'm not sure which exactly because this elevator only has two stops- the lobby and his office. Kyle seems unaffected by all of this but to me, this is straight ballin'. If this was my elevator, it would only play *Stairway to Heaven*.

Maybe *Flight of the Valkyries*. Get some fucking bombast up in this bitch.

We get out and enter what appears to be a waiting room, except there's a motherfucking waterfall in it. Inside a skyscraper, downtown, there's a waterfall INSIDE a waiting room.

Sensing that I'm on the verge of being overwhelmed, Kyle pushes me into a chair and says, "Relax, Will. Don't let this get to you. This whole thing," he says while waving across the room, "is just to get inside people's head. It gives him leverage. He's not gunning for you so just relax."

In what sounds like it must be an intercom we hear, "Sir will see you now. Please enter through the lighted doorway." And just then, a doorway on the other side of the room lights up. Like, the wood is glowing or something. I don't see any lights or bulbs or LEDs but there's no denying the doorway is in fact lit.

Not nearly enough pills for this.

If the waiting room was overwhelming decadence, this guy's office is walking through the Pearly Gates to find heaven is a strip club of all supermodels and the champagne room is free. Ivory is everywhere. Half of the stuff is gold leaf but doesn't look tacky, just expensive and tasteful. There's two of those massive floor-to-ceiling bookshelves stacked with hundreds of old, leather bound books. This is like if the Smithsonian did a room in overwhelming elegance.

"Gentlemen, please take a seat." I hadn't seen anyone, but right in plain sight, behind a massive oak desk, is an older man, early sixties probably, hand extended towards a leather sofa.

I am yet to find a single light source in this room but it's so well lit.

"So, do I call you William, or do I call you John?

"Well, my pay check says 'William' so…". I hear Kyle exhale.

"So John it is then. And feel free to call me Mr. Marianio."

So this is what it feels like to lose a dick measuring contest. Got it.

"John, I'm hearing good things about you. You're pissing off people. I like that."

"Sir?" I am completely unaware of pissed off people. Maybe I should blow him or something?

"The religious nut jobs, the hairy-legged feminists groups. The right people to piss off. The fucking losers. The idiots who not only don't realize their lame cause is dead on arrival but by protesting and boycotting and sending emails to the local news, are only fueling the fire."

"Mr. Marianio, I wasn't aware I was bothering anyone with my show. I have the utmost respect for the religious, I'd never-"

"John, son. You did a show on sex toy disasters. How did you think that would sit with Ma and Pa Bible Belt?"

"I guess I didn't?" Kyle is shooting daggers at me with his eyes. Well, screw him, he could have prepped me for this. "I can tone is down some, Mr. Marianio."

"Fuck that, and fuck them. Personally, I think your show is horse shit. But it brings the numbers, it brings the ratings, and you are single handedly expanding our online empire. I love you, John. I love your shitty show."

I'm not thinking Ringing Endorsement but I can't blame you if you were.

"You keep being you, Boo-boo. Hey, I like that. That's your new nickname. Boo-boo. Anyway, fuck what they think, fuck what I think. You bring me numbers. I want numbers like viewership percentages. Numbers after dollar signs. And now more than ever, and this is new shit for me to give a flying fuck about, numbers after web views. You are gonna be alright, John." Whew.

"Now that we got that clear, Kyle, get out of my office."

"Hey, wait a minute. I represent him. I'm to be around all negotiation, even informal conversations. You know the laws on this."

"There's no damned negotiation. I'm allowed to talk to my talent and give them advice. Career mentorship. If only you had had some, huh?"

Kyle is obviously pissed but I give that not-subtle-at-all head shake and he grudgingly leaves the room.

"Okay, John, we need to have a conversation about cocaine."

"Sir?"

"Cocaine, John. The white stuff you snort. Coke."

"Sir?" What is this? If I didn't know what to say when my dad asked me in high school if I smoked pot, I sure as hell can't handle this. I don't think he can piss test me so Plan A is to lie lie lie.

"Don't lie to me, either." Well fuck.

"Sir, I'm not sure what you are talking about."

"Oh for fuck's sake. John, I have coke residue on this desk older than you." Okay then. "So where do you get your flake?"

"Umm, I don't know, actually, I have an assistant who get s it for me."

"Wait. You buy down, not up?"

"Huh? Sir, I mean, huh?"

"You let someone under you score your flake? That's just stupid. Why aren't you using your name to obtain the premium shit?"

"Sir, I can't get caught with a few ounces and definitely can't get caught copping a quarter pound."

"First, no more buying in fractions. There's no restraint with coke. Don't bottle yourself into false restrictions. Second, you do your buying yourself. Don't be a pussy. Look, the part timers buying an eight ball on a Friday, that's not our league. That's fantasy football. You and I play in the NFL. Shit, they aren't even fantasy football. They're that magnetic game that bounces the pieces around from back in the seventies. Fuck them. Think big league. Be big league."

"Big league. Got it, sir."

"So where is your flake coming from?"

"Bolivia."

"They tell you that?"

I nod my head north and south.

"Then you are getting shit or you're getting lied to."

Or, knowing Josh, both.

"There hasn't been any good Bolivian on the east coast in eight years now. That shit gets funneled to Europe through narco-terrorists. They sell it as environmental coke. Those pussy-ass libs in Europe love them some environmental bullshit and pay a premium that makes the Atlantic shipment a non-issue.

No, if you are getting good shit, it's probably Peruvian, possibly Ecuadorian. But if they are telling you it's Bolivian, you are getting Venezuela's middle tier shit. Their middle finger. You can do better. Here," he says, sliding me a business card. "Call this guy. Tell him you know me and he owes you a lunch. It'll happen from there. And John."

"Yes sir?"

"Don't send a bullshit lackey to pick up an order. Not for a few months. Make a relationship. Make a friend."

"Got it."

"So did Kyle tell you I was trying to intimidate you, get in your head?"

"He said something about that, yes."

"Well, you did good. Most first time new-to-fame guys, when I tell them they are pissing people off, offer to blow me."

30

Today is our weekly production meeting. I have to imagine there are worse places to be but for the life of me, I can't think of one right now. This is where we fine-tune the eight episodes we are going to tape this week. Schedule is: Monday, plan the shows. Then, tape two a day for the rest of the week. This way, we have our shows banked. Sometimes we work week-on/ week-off. We usually tape all of October and early November and then don't tape until after the new year. We don't get a true summer break like sitcoms or dramas or CSI: Salt Lake City so we tape a lot in March, April, and May so we have plenty of downtime in the summer. We are responsible for forty-two weeks of shows per year. So that's twenty-one weeks of balls to the wall taping every year. It may be a lot of sex and drugs, but it's still a job.

We don't just map out the week cartography style, but we are also brainstorming. Trying to set up ideas for shows moving forward. Conceptual stuff. Trying to find themes that fit the time they will air. Setting up guests. You can't just throw together *Gay Transgendered Love Triangles* in a week. It takes hard work and commitment.

Granted, none of that hard work or commitment comes from me, which is why there are a dozen or so other people in the room. Josh is the only one whose name I actually know. The rest are pet names I make up as I go.

Blonde Perky Boobs speaks up and says we may want to push *Lobotomized Health Care Providers* because they're apparently a rare fucking breed and we can't fake this one because they'll need to show the scar.

"We can't fake a fucking scar? Is make-up that pathetic? That's insane, pun not intended," I say indignantly.

But Blonde Perky Boobs is adamant that the demo market for this show, which shares a chunk of the Venn diagram with cutters, are way into this and can identify a fake scar a mile away.

"We can just shoot what we have this week, and hold the tape for when an episode runs short," Josh interjects. This is probably best as a short add-in segment as I'm bored talking about it, there's probably not much ass to be had from it, and I can't begin to figure out the pill cocktail it would take to interview lobotomized people.

They are also having problems finding coke head stripper moms. UNACCEPTABLE.

"If you pieces of dog excrement can't find the very elemental basis for this show, I will replace you with someone who can!" Deep breath. Deep breath. These motherfuckers are straight fucking with my emotions. I'm irate on a very personal level right now.

Sensing this, Cheap Haircut and Worse Cologne pipes in with, "Well, we are set on a themed sexual deviants week in about a month." That's coming through for a brother right there.

"Details, good man. Details." There's no need to blueball me, man. Guy Code 101.

"Well, plenty of nympho teachers. Umm, probably a full show on being addicting to sex work. Still coming up short on strippers but we can hire actresses so no biggie." There is a biggie. They are likely to not be cokeheads, but we can work around that. It's not like actresses say no to the D. "We have assorted perversion... can only lay pipe in a church... some light groupsex drama... World War II roleplaying..."

I'm not thinking Bombing Pearl Harbor but I can't blame you if you were.

"... shopping mall exhibitionism... the normal weird shit."

Cheap Haircut and Worse Cologne saves the day.

"We need to get a theme and market the fuck out it. This needs to be a special week," I tell my team. Special for TV, special for my sex life. Special. "What else have we got?"

Shitty Tie looks around, deliberately not looking at me. "Well, sir, the thing is... we've reached a kind of market saturation on sex." Impossible. Lies. "Ratings are down for the 'normal' stuff and we're running low anyways, and more deviant stuff is either harder to come by or illegal." Technicalities. "We are looking at adding more mental illness stuff, and transgender is hot right now but gay stuff is way down- probably too mainstream- and as we already discussed, we are bottoming out on strippers, especially the cokeheads. I did find a pretty whacked out stripper in a custody fight with an MMA fighter... but I'm pretty sure she's *ahem* mob protected now so there will be no... *extracurriculars.*"

That's just bullshit. This is like a college application. I don't care what your grades are, show me the extracurriculars.

Less Eagle Scout, more down with anal. Less double plays on the softball team and more double penetration for my balls. Less missionary work and more missionary position. Dog shelter versus doggy style.

This meeting is a complete buzz kill so I confirm the schedule for the week and walk out, leaving a room full of unsure faces.

■ ■ ■

"Today on *TalkShowX*, Complicated Love Triangles! And now, John Sterling!"

The applause is deafening as I walk out from behind the partition that makes up the back wall of the stage. I have a shit-eating grin on, mostly because of the Lithium and Pamalor, but the fact that my ratings are up 12% doesn't hurt much. I gesture to the audience to calm down, to be seated.

"Thank you. Thank you everyone. Today's show is going to be a great one. We have some of the most convoluted, complicated love triangles I have seen in my entire life." More applause. "First, let's have Emily come out." A slight blonde walks out, dressed in Lycra head to toe, big hair teased up with what looks like a gallon of hairspray. She is pretty enough to fuck after the show, but knowing what I know about her,

I wouldn't stick my dick in her with twelve rubbers on. Not even oral, and that says a lot. "So, Emily, tell us about your boyfriend Michael." It takes her a couple of seconds to process this request.

"Well. Mikey and I have been seeing each other for around two years now. We've been talking about marriage for awhile now, but we keep putting it off."

"Why is that Emily?" I should win a damn Oscar for acting like I care about this.

"Well, I have been seeing someone else, someone I care a lot about, too." A few quick groans fly through the audience. It doesn't take a rocket scientist to figure out whom it is. "His brother Bobby." The audience goes ballistic. We didn't even have to flash the "applause" sign. Normally, the mongoloids in the crowd can never figure out when they should make noise.

"Are you...sleeping with him?"

"Of course I am. I got to figure out who I want to be with forever, right? It's like a test drive. Leasing with the option to buy." Right.

"Is Bobby the only guy you're test driving?"

Emily goes on to tell us all about the four other guys she's leasing right now. That's six in total. And does she use protection, you might ask. Of course not. Birth control? Of course not. Does she have more than eight brain cells?

Of course not.

Three minutes later, we have Michael on stage. He's a big guy, over six feet tall, medium build, but muscular, just like most mechanics. He has an easy smile, but blank eyes. He can't be too bright, dating Emily and all.

"So, Mike, do you have any idea why Emily brought you here today?"

"Naw sir, no idea'r. But I'mma make somethin' of it, sure am. Got a few things I been needin' to tell Em and this here's as good a place as any in the holler."

"Fair enough Mike, but it's Emily's turn first. Emily, what did you want to say to your boyfriend?"

"Mikey, we've been seeing each other for awhile and we're talking about getting hitched up some day and I love you with all my heart, but..."

"But you're fuckin' Bobby. That about right?" He sprouted a huge, dumb smile. "Shit, girl, I knowed all along. He tol' me right after that there first time at Gary's. That, uhhh Christmas bash. Hell, I was the one who tol' him it was cool."

The audience is going nuts at this. A guy wearing a Harley t-shirt calls her a slut and him a pimp. I can't quite argue with that.

We bring Bobby out, and him and his brother exchange high-fives and laugh and point at Emily, who is now on the verge of tears.

Return three minutes later, after a commercial break brought to you by I Can't Believe It's Not Butter, Ford Trucks, and Chia Pets.

I am talking. "Now, Emily, you asked us to run a pregnancy test for you because you were a little behind in your monthly visitor." It wasn't a lie, but she already knew the results. It's kind of hard to hide the fact that not only are you pregnant, but with twins when doing an ultrasound with amniocentesis for genetic testing. But, theatrics and my charm and the audience will believe anything. "Some unknown man whom we didn't test is the father. For those at home, we tested five men. FIVE."

You'd think that Eddie Murphy was doing his James Brown impersonation the way the audience exploded with laughter. They even began to chant "whore" and "dumb slut." And I wonder why I get no recognition as a humanitarian.

"Six guys. Damn, Emily, don't you ever say no? Christ, keep those legs closed, no one wants a whiff, anyway." At least Michael is showing some emotion. Bobby seems on the verge of falling asleep. The worst part about the whole thing is this is the time I really did lie. According to the test, it's 93% that Michael is the father. But chicks knocked up by their boyfriend doesn't boost viewership anywhere except maybe in Utah or some shit. I'd feel bad, but the chemicals make that pretty difficult.

Emily storms off the set in tears, followed by a barrage of taunts and laughter.

It's not like they'll never figure it out. They knew this was about entertainment and they know the reputation of *TalkShowX*. You may think that we have some obligation to honesty and offering correct information. If that's what you think, you should get a clamp and hydraulic jack to help you get your head out of your ass.

My producer tells me this all about entertainment. This all about making the average American feel better about his place in the world. This is about grabbing attention and delivering conflict.

Consider it delivered, Mr. Average American.

31

Brandi is one of those cheerful, happy, dots-her-i's-with-tiny-hearts kind of girls and you feel a deep sense of profound personal nirvana when she gets shit on.

Figuratively, of course. Literally is a whole different story.

She's backstage. "Happy to meet you! It's great to be here in New York! I just love New York! Isn't it just a GREAT day today?" Oh yeah, Brandi, everything's just peachy fucking keen. See, she thinks she's going to propose to her boyfriend, Eric. She doesn't realize today's show doesn't have a matrimonial theme to say the least. Today's show- Cyber Porn.

The way this happened is Josh comes into my office two months ago. "Yo, John, you have got to check this out." He stood a step inside my doorway and looked at me.

"Check what out?" Josh was a little slow in the mornings.

"Your email. I forwarded it to you. I think we got a live one here."

I tapped the fake little pseudo mousepad to wake up my laptop and logged on. I opened a forward from Josh and quickly read the email. It was from some kid in the suburbs of Chicago. He knows his girlfriend has been sending letters to the show because she wants to go on the show and propose to him. Now, Eric doesn't want to marry this girl-Brandi- and he just happens to have a website he'd like to reveal to her on air.

I click the link. Eight seconds later, 6 jpegs pop up, with what looks like pictures of various young ladies orally pleasuring the same johnson.

I'm not thinking Ex-fiancée but I can't blame you if you were.

What happens next is we "find" one of Brandi's letters and respond. We phone interview her and arrange for her and her boyfriend to come to New York for two days. This really is shooting big, dumb fish in a very tiny barrel.

On stage, Brandi is pretty much all deer in headlights, with the lights and cameras and audience and the battery for her mike strapped across the small of her back like explosives. She's stammering a little bit, and though I know in all my infinite wisdom that's she's just a little nervous, she's coming off as stupid.

Brandi thinks it's "rad" to pop the question on *TalkShowX*, it makes it "real on the inside."

Yeah, well, we're all gonna be a lot more familiar with Brandi's insides in, like, eight minutes.

I'm not thinking Dildo Cam but I can't blame you if you were.

Fast forward about seven minutes later, after Eric rejects Brandi's sweet and heartfelt proposal. Fast forward through

Brandi's tears, foggy and salty, rolling down her cheeks. Fast forward though just another stupid chemical reaction.

It isn't the Tupac t-shirt Eric's wearing that let's you know it's going to get good. It's not the Puma sneakers with the extra thick laces, but I guess it helps. Call it a small world and all, but I had those same sneakers when I was 7. It's not even Eric's usage of the word "pimpin'" that should set off the flares. No, it has to be the ferocity in which he grabs his genitals. We're talking intensity like a mother fucking supernova.

Eric and Brandi proceed to argue back and forth, half of the conversation getting bleeped out. During a lull in the fracas, a security guy rolls out a table with a computer on it.

With this, the audience erupts with a burst of "CY-BER-PORN!" All Eric can seem to say is "Yea, now what, bitch?" but the way he says it, it sounds more like "beach."

Brandi looks confused, but then again, I think she looks confused quite a bit.

Eric tells Brandi there's a website she should check out. He points to the mouse and says click it, as if it was a dare or something. Keep in mind that the computer is hooked up to all the monitors in the studio. We're greeted with what is apparently Eric's cock in the mouth and/or faces of eight or nine different girls, none of which are Brandi.

To say Brandi went ballistic would be sheer understatement. It's truly difficult to scream at the top of your lungs when you're crying that much, but she did a stellar job of it. She was trying hard to hit Eric though the intervening security guard.

I'm not thinking Straight To Video but I can't blame you if you were.

Eric's defense was noble, though. "But they're only pictures. I only post movies of the girl I love." For a brief second, I think Brandi thought this was a compliment, but slowly, the color ran out of her face. By the time Eric's hand reached for the mouse and his finger raised to come down on the button, she was as white as chalk.

What happens next is a two minute movie, shot from the standard "Piston" view. Slowly, the camera moves across what is clearly Eric and we see the girl, who is clearly Brandi.

You might not guess it by looking at her, but Brandi just loves to have "that fat meat all stuffed up in me."

■ ■ ■

There's a knock on my door and before I can say come in, Josh bounds through like it's his office. He drops a baggie of a fine white powder in front of me and stares vacantly out my large window with a view of the skyline.

"Anything else, Josh? You mixing barbiturates again?" Josh has developed this nasty habit, which he refers to as "stupidfying" himself, of snorting a line, taking a handful of various barbs, and washing them down with Tanqueray. It didn't effect his work, per say, but it can't be good for him in the long haul.

"Um. Yeah. I mean, no, not stupidfied. But, yeah, there was something else. Hmmm. Oh that guy called." Oh really? Thanks Josh.

"Ok Josh, I need a little more information. Name, phone number, message. These things would be helpful."

"Yeah. I have a message right here." He hands me a piece of paper with a name on it. James Walters 555-7658.

"Thanks Josh. I'll see you in post-pro, around 3. And Josh, lay off the nose candy a little. You're getting pretty fucked up." He nods, either knowingly or totally oblivious to his surroundings. I vote on oblivion, but that might just be what I prefer.

James Walters is a rep from this merchandising company that wants to put out John Sterling t-shirts and bumper stickers. He even has mentioned action figures. You too could be the proud owner of a 6-inch me, or any of our four insanely popular security men, as well as a cameraman (complete with moving camera!) and a few generalized guests. We don't own the rights to images or likenesses of our guests, but face it, they all look the same after three episodes. He is pretty sure Sgt. Shock will allow a figure of him. There will also be a set you can buy that will come with movable furniture (easier to throw that way) and an audience complete with seating.

I pick up my phone and call James back. He offers me five digits to let this happen. The lawyers have seen the paperwork and they think it's fine. He thinks it will outsell the action figures from that new slasher flick with teen nudity. You know the one, the female lead has big breasts and everyone gets killed.

I think it is disturbing that people would let their children buy action figures to re-enact such crappy shows. Animal Pornography. I'm Married To An Escort Girl. Clergy With STDs.

Look, mommy, the college roommates are beating each other up 'cause one filmed the other showering and posted it on the Internet. I can even throw a chair!

James asks me if I've given even further thought about t-shirts. Bumper stickers. Coffee mugs with catchy slogans. A 16-month calendar. He can see it now. All of America will be draped in t-shirts proclaiming "Sterling for Prez." Cars around the country will have stickers on them touting "Sterling is God." People all over the world will drink their morning coffee in mugs with the show's logo and say "Liquid Crack" on them.

This may be getting out of hand but my bills are getting paid on time for the first time in years.

I tell James to forward the contract for the action figures to my lawyers and to fax a proposal for the other stuff. I give Brian a call at the bookstore to see ho this trip to Amsterdam was, but the girl who answers says Brian is off today and got back eight months ago. I wonder out loud if she's sleeping with him and she hangs up loudly.

32

I'm taping today's show- Hardcore Fetishes. I'm talking to a middle aged couple from the Midwest who have been married for nine years, happily, I might add, Gina and Roger. They claim to have a happy sex life. So how often do they have sex? Ten times a week? Five? Thirty?

Try zero. None. Nine years, no penetration.

Why is that? Well, Roger has this voyeur fetish. He likes to watch the object of his sexual desire have sex with strange men.

Which is cool with Gina because she's an exhibitionist. Their sex goes like this:

Pick up strange guy in a chat room or swinger web site.

Meet him in hotel room.

Roger stands in closet and whacks off into the bath robe you can take home for $30, while a strange man fucks his wife.

I'm not thinking Golden Age of Courting but I can't blame you if you were.

Gina has actually never even seen Roger's penis. Ever. Her husband of nine years.

After them, we have your standard S&M people, a chick who's into bondage a little more than necessary, and a couple addicted to public sex. Your basic sex fetish stuff, nothing you can't find on the internet, you know.

Somehow taping ran quick today and I had to shoot another additional segment, one I hadn't prepped for. I walk backstage and Josh is standing there, smiling widely. Laughing under his breath, he hands me a note card and says to have fun.

I look at the card. *Nathan Woods: 29: Recycler.* That's it. Name, age, and "recycler", what ever that means. Sounds like a shitty comic book hero to me.

I'm back on stage, the crowd applauds and we're back. I introduce Nathan and he comes out and sits down.

"Now, Nathan," I say, "it says here that you're 29 and a … recycler. What's that mean, you recycle your cans?"

"No, John, it's a little different than cans, but not by much. It refers to… well, how I spank it. Sorta."

"And recycling relates to masturbation how exactly?"

"Well, I recycle the by-product."

"How in the world do you recycle an orgasm?" What did Josh do now?

"No, no- the seed. I recycle the seed."

"Huh? How do you recycle jizz?"

"By consuming it, so it may come forth again."

"So what you're saying is you eat your semen?"

"Well, yes. By recycling the holy seed, I keep it holy, instead of wasting my seed of life."

And, ladies and gentlemen, he has a special way for this. When he climaxes, he shoots into an old pickle jar, which he saves and refrigerates until it's full. Then, well, he drinks it. Straight, no chaser.

I'm about to puke when we finally wrap and Josh is lying on the floor, laughing his ass off, tears streaming down his face.

■ ■ ■

I cancelled my shrink appointment today. It's the fifth straight one I've cancelled. I'm not what you call Committed to Therapy anymore. There's no more Dedication to Excellence coming from me. No Desire for Perfection. Not even a smidge of Aiming for a Better Life.

Kyle Wennington, my beloved agent, calls me at home.

Why aren't you at work?

Why didn't you show up at the Billboard Award Ceremony last night?

Have you ever heard of biting the hand that feeds you? Does the phrase Media Darling mean anything to you? Am I doing this all by myself?

Are you doing the drinking again?

I haven't touched a drop in weeks. Months. Outside of coke and pills, I have been clean. I haven't drank in months. My body is a temple and I like to have it worshipped, daily, by strange new women.

Kyle tells me that he received a contract for the action figures, as well as one for a board game. That's not a typo. I said board game. Some company wants to turn my five hours a week of mind destroying cancer into a play-at-home, fun-for-the-whole-family- board game. And I sound like I have a drinking problem? There wasn't an outline for the game, but I can just see it now.

Daddy landed on the Moral Abyss space, so he has to either roll doubles or lose two grams of cocaine.

I worry about the people who need a play-at-home version. Isn't watching at home bad enough?

Kyle tells me I need to sign off on the action figures. I need to stop by his office, I'm being sued. It's totally groundless, he tells me. It's not my fault some little girl in Iowa started to strip for her class. I'm not the moral police, he tells me.

He tells me this is just a victimless crime.

"It's unavoidable. People are just looking for a scapegoat. A pariah. Someone to take the fall, baby."

I try to tell him I've already fallen. I try to tell him I need a ladder to see the depths of depression. Like Kyle ever listens to me. I'm just his meal ticket.

I hang up and try to go back to sleep. And then the phone rings again. And it's Brian. He wants to know what's new. He saw yesterday's show and it was hilarious.

I try to tell him that nothing's new. Nothing is ever new. I'm just wasting my life, televising human devolution. He tells me he has tickets to a concert, some band we used to like back in college.

It's the same night as some Tibetan benefit I said I'd speak at. Like my words matter to them. It's how many zeros are on the check.

My hands are shaking so I tell Brian I have to take a wicked shit but I'll call him back later. I take five or six Percocets and go back to sleep, haunted by black, smoky dreams.

33

Today's show- *Who's The Daddy?*

These shows aren't that bad, but today, all of our confused mothers are underage. The prison demographic skyrockets for this.

Lindsey is 15 and not sure which of three guys impregnated her. It could be Billy, who is 15, Travis, who is 17 or Marty, who is, hold your breath, 34. My first thought was statutory rape but we're dealing with Texans here, so I think it's only a $75 fine.

Lindsey's parents are hoping it's Travis, because "at least he's been a-holdin' down a job." If you call the towel boy at a car wash a job. None of the guys seems poised for fatherhood, but if any of these guys could cut the old paternal cake, it would have to be Travis. He's the only one who speaks in complete sentences. Marty can't go four words without saying "um...well...um." Shakespeare is rolling in his grave.

Of the three, she's had more sex with Billy, who was her boyfriend for five months, forever to the high school crowd.

Of course, Billy denies paternity because he used to make her douche with soda after they copulated.

Not just any soda, but Mr. Pibb. We all know about Mr. Pibb's contraceptive properties.

I'm not thinking New Coke but I can't blame you if you were.

And we'd love to tell you who the father is, but first, you should meet Debbie. Debbie is a freshman at the University of Oklahoma. Debbie had a few too many at a frat party and suddenly turned into a pussy-buffet. Her friends tell her that she did the nasty with at least thirty guys, but they didn't keep count after she passed out. They just left.

Some friends.

Guys were taking numbers to fuck this girl. A fight broke out over whether or not to violate her anus. And they thought her dignity was preserved when no one became a sodomite.

The silver lining, for Debbie perhaps, was that she had a raging gonorrhea infection before that fateful weekend. Guess they should have gone anal, huh?

Note to all men at U of O- see a doctor ASAP.

We can't help Debbie find out who her offspring's father is, but before we tell you about the dramatic conclusion to her story, please welcome Jenna to the show.

Jenna is 16 and not sure which of four gentlemen suitors planted their seed in her egg. None of the four potential fathers, by the way, is her boyfriend. She's waiting until marriage to sleep with him.

And they say morals are on the decline.

And the four guys? You guessed it, two groups of brothers. I guess Jenna just likes to keep it in the family.

It's not like these girls are made up either. This show is true reality. These girls did this. These guys (at least some of them) did it to them. I'm what you call a facilitator. I'm trying to get what you call closure. I'm just looking forward to what you call group sex with consenting adult women.

And people think I'm a hero.

If you need to know, Lindsey got knocked up by Billy, who is going to drop out of school to support the child. Debbie's fetus, a girl, does not have gonorrhea. And lovely Jenna didn't get knocked up by any of the four boys. It was, hold your breath now, her cousin. Like I said, keep it in the family. Hey, at least it was a second cousin. Anything else would be gross.

This is my world. And the ratings are through the roof. I am now in every major market in North America. I can be viewed in 97% of the USA. I am the top rated show in both prisons and mental institutes. I will easily make over half a million dollars this year, more with foreign syndication and those freaking action figures.

I now have three websites dedicated to my adoration. I receive eight thousand pieces of fan mail a day. Over one hundred marriage proposals. Scores of nude pictures. The occasional video.

I am Jesus' kid brother. And as always, when Jesus' kid brother is dealing with underage girls, Sgt. Shock storms out.

"What in the hell do we have here? You, girl (pointing to Lindsey) what in God's green Earth are you doing, doing a 30 something year old man? You ain't nothing but a wee little girl.

Where's your momma when you're bumpin' the nasties with this pervert? He's a damn senior citizen in your eyes!"

The audience explodes like Hiroshima.

"And you, giving the disease to all those poor boys. Why didn't you tell them you were a skank?"

"But I passed out!"

Time for audience stupidity.

"No wonder she's got an STD, doin' thirty guys like that!"

"If that was my daughter, I'd send her to a convent, *if* they'd take her sorry ass."

"They should take her baby away before she sells if for crack." Right. For crack.

34

Brainstorm meeting with production so it must be a Monday. It seems that we're running out of truly wonderful ideas and ratings aren't going up anymore. They haven't begun the decline just yet, but that could happen any day now. What we need are some great ideas to bring those viewers over from the rival shows.

Some new girl, a blonde I've never seen before, who looks like an amazing fuck, says we should do something heart warming. Unite a family. Do an intervention. Inspire our viewers. I'm going to venture to guess she missed our Crackhead Grandmothers show. It was as inspiring as a swift kick to the groin.

Maybe we should bring back popular past guests, Josh recommends. We could check in on them and manage to steal whatever dignity they left with. Wonderful idea. In fact, it's such a good idea we tried before Josh came on board. Turned out no one wanted to come back. The only people who seemed interested were totally lame. People with the life and vibrancy of a rotting vegetable. Zucchini, Indian corn, a small legume, it doesn't matter as long as it's rotting.

No, no, no, says Josh, we can liven them up. That's not a problem. It's all in the presentation. Smoke and mirrors. An optical illusion. You just need to add spice to that old recipe. Flash and dash.

These people could dry paint with their personalities and Josh swears they will be as entertaining as Gangbang Survivors. Transfigured Teachers and the Classes Who Love Them.

I say we need another Cokehead Stripper Mom show. There is no better blowjob than one from an adult performer who is lactating.

With all due respect to mothers.

Of course.

Josh tells me he's going to get right on this. He wants a list of all our past guests and he'll start calling them this afternoon. He's on the job, he's got the plan down cold. The ball's in his court and he's going to run with it.

I head back to my office to read the biographies of today's guests. Before I can settle in, my mother is on the phone wanting to talk to me.

I pick up and say hello.

"Why don't you ever call me?" Because you are a reminder of failure, mother dearest.

"So have you met any nice women?"

With my job, there's not many nice women around.

"Will you be coming by the house for dinner anytime soon? I miss you so."

My heart is tearing into two pieces here. If I'm not careful, I just might shed a tear.

Just one, though.

Look, Mom, I've got to run, I'm so busy here, what with the show and promotional stuff going on. You know, I have a new promo head I have to train and make sure everything is OK with the job and all that stuff so I've got to go, I'll talk to you soon, bye-bye, click.

■ ■ ■

What the show Josh has planned is what we call in the business *exploitation*. It's recycling trash that in all honesty should be buried forty miles below the crust of the Earth in a concrete lined well like nuclear waste. This is the accident on the side of the road, the mangled corpse at the end of the thirty feet of bloody skid mark that you cannot look at. It's that part of you that says "This tastes horrible. Here, you try." It's that sick part of human nature that wants others to suffer the same abuse as you.

Your high school math teacher lied to you. He told you that any time you had a fraction with one as the denominator, it was the lowest common denominator.

Wrong. This, this right here, this is the lowest common denominator.

But at least there are going to be tons of viewers. We've been advertising this show for three weeks now. During our show, late at night, during the day when most people work but our viewers are home, doing whatever worthless things they do to suck more time into their void.

It's not that I don't like my viewers. I just have no respect for them.

We've spent more on this show than we do on any given ten episodes. It only takes one total debacle to keep people from watching for a month. It's about carnage and Josh is adamant we will deliver this. He calls it "better television through chemicals."

I think I know what he is up to, but I really don't want to get involved in this.

We've got two KKK guys coming back, a cokehead stripper mom (yes!), her mother and two daughters, a transgendered couple, a handful of blacks and Latinos for the KKK to embarrass themselves in front of, a rather corpulent exotic dancer, two sisters and the man they share, a man addicted to child pornography, and, of course, Sgt. Shock. Wouldn't be abomination unto broadcasting without him. We also have a few underage criminals for him to confront if things don't go as planned.

But here's the thing that's so freaking wonderful about this. We're doing it live, with only a seven second delay. We'll have the black box handy, which for some odd reason is not black nor a box. It's a red button, but that sends the message of nuclear holocaust. We won't be able to blur out any nudity, should that arise (and please not from the fat stripper) so we'll have to black box that out.

It's going to be cutting edge television, a trend-setting program with ramifications that will far outlast the show. It will make the annals of television.

And I'm having this gut feeling that this will be a horrible, horrible mistake, I swear to God.

Meh. Nothing dicyclomine can't take care of.

■ ■ ■

I'm not sure why they call the Green Room the Green Room because the walls are oyster white and the carpets are that deep blue that won't show the dirt or a coffee spill or a cigarette burn. Imperial True Blue, that's the color. Still, it's the Green Room, and all of our guests are in there, waiting to come out for the show. We have deli sandwiches out, as well as water and coffee to drink.

The sandwiches are either turkey with American cheese, or tuna salad.

I am chitchatting with Josh and one of the guys from editing, having the guests come up and tell me just how much they love my show, blah, blah, blah. Josh tells me that his plan has been implemented and there's only three minutes until the show begins. The guests start to file out into the corridor where they'll wait to be called out for the show. This is when Josh tells me his plan: putting industrial strength speed in their drinks. Not the normal trace amounts bullshit either. Nope, not that. Mass quantities. And it's not just speed. There's also a mild combination of steroids and some hallucinogenic chemical used to combat vertigo. It's tasteless and odorless. Josh says they should be real live wires out there. He just put it in their drink when he got it for them.

Because the one guy from the KKK had a history of abusing speed, and therefore a higher tolerance, he tripled his amount when he put it in his tea.

But Josh, I say, the guys from the KKK all had water. The only person drinking tea was the grandmother.

"No, they drank tea, the grandmother had the coffee."

"No Josh, she didn't. She can't have coffee due to a hypersensitivity to stimulants. It's right on her fucking bio card. Stimulants of *any* kind are severely harmful to her."

"Oh shit. She drank the tea with a boatload of speed in it."

"Josh, we need to call an ambulance. She's gonna fucking die on national television."

"No, what we need to do is get rid of any evidence. Get every trace of anything illegal out of this building now. We're going to have to act like we didn't go a thing. Do you realize how much trouble we'll be in?"

Am I familiar with attempted manslaughter?

Do I know what fifty to life means?

Do I like violent ass rape?

Am I ready to lose everything I have just to save this woman?

Well, as they say, the show must go on.

Eight minutes later, grandma is on stage, sweating like a woman in labor. Why did I want to start off with Cokehead Stripper Mom, anyway? She could have just as easily died backstage.

I'm not thinking Instant Karma but I can't blame you if you were.

Everyone probably thinks she's just sweating from either nervousness or from the zillion watt lights we have. Or both. Me, I don't sweat because of the lighting anymore, thanks to Glandnex. All sweating does is regulate body temperature and help in the removing of impurities. When your piss is the deep brown of some Oktoberfest beer and your bowel movements are solid black square chunks of recycled dinner and your phlegm glows in the dark, it's safe to say all impurities are getting out somehow.

Fifteen minutes later, good old grandma is as dead as a bait kitten.

A bait kitten is a kitten used by big game fishermen to catch a truly large fish. If you want a sailfish, use a coon cat. A swordfish calls for a calico longhair. It it's a shark you're after, just cut the neck of any cat and toss it over.

You don't want to know how I know this.

You can't hook it through the neck, because it'll die too quickly. The blood can easily backup in its lungs and it'll drown in blood before it drowns from the water or is eaten. You want it to be alive for as long as possible. It's the desperate flailing that attracts the fish.

A good place to hook it is through the thigh of one of it's back legs. Less likely to damage a major organ. This encourages both maximum bleeding and movement before being crunched down the throat of a predatory species that looks great as a trophy.

And grandma is that dead.

35

There's that big, dramatic gasp by everyone in the building when the producer takes his hand from her neck and says, "I can't feel a pulse. I think... she's dead."

I hope that by now, we're to commercial.

People start running all over the place, like winning a marathon will bring her back to life. There are about a million people on their cell phones, but how many are calling 911 and how many are calling friends to tell them, I don't know. Half the people are massed around the body, the evidence, and the other half are huddled just in front of the stage.

Josh walks up behind me quickly and whispers in my ear "Shit, man, I gotta get rid of some shit. I'll be right back."

"No way. Where do you think you're going? We have to tell the cops what happened. You can't tamper with evidence."

"Do you want to go to jail? Do you know what they do to skinny white guys in jail? The reality of the situation is we need to get rid of everything. Everything right now."

"Uh, I have some coke in my desk that can go with you then, please?"

His eyes all bugged out, he nods back and mouths a *yeah*.

A minute after Josh leaves, the first cops show up. The first person they want to speak with is me, and the first thing they say is what big fans they are. Next, they want to know what happened.

I didn't see it, I tell them, I was in the audience. Pointing off stage, I say, her family's back there. By now, there's more cops and they're trying to disperse the crowd but the people, they aren't going anywhere. Even when the firefighters show up, no one is giving up prime real estate.

Slightly dazed, and definitely overmedicated, I wander into my office, and there's Josh, putting tape after tape into a cardboard box. It takes me a minute, but then I realize these are the tapes of us screwing all those chicks.

Getting head.

Doing drugs.

Group sex, gangbang, multiple partners, what ever you want to call it.

"Man," Josh says, "we have got to get out of here. If they find these, we are totally dead. Fucking jail bait, man."

Just when I'm about to ask what the hell he's freaking over, a cop ducks his head in and reminds that we need to go down to the station pronto to give a statement.

"We have got to ditch town, man. We're going to jail big time."

No way, I say. How can they link this to us? You got rid of the "evidence", right?

He tells me he flushed it.

Then what's the problem? We're fine.

"Not really. They probably already have search warrants because we're famous so really we can't get these tapes out. Plus, there's more, well, more, um, *white* around here than is legal."

"You didn't get rid of all of it?"

"Fucker, you never asked why there was always a bump within three seconds before, don't start now."

What do we do then, I ask.

Josh tells me we need to get out of town, to let things die down a little, get our stories straight. He says they might find a scapegoat.

He tells me to meet him at a car rental place near the airport in three hours, he needs to get some things ready. Don't, he reminds me, use an ATM. They trace you that way. No large cash withdrawals.

I guess, in retrospect, that this is where we crossed that line.

■ ■ ■

I thought about going back to my apartment to get some stuff but was afraid that maybe the police had it staked out. Not knowing where to go, I went to Stephen's.

I knocked on his door and waited. Neil answered and let me in.

"What's going?" he asks me.

Oh, not much really. A little murder, some drug offenses, nothing, really.

My brother comes in to say hi and I ask if they've been watching the news. They say no. Good, I tell them, don't watch that shit right now. Bad vibes, I tell them.

They look at each other weird, meaning I'm being weird. Can you blame me?

"Are you ok? What's wrong?"

Don't ask me that, I say. I just need a favor. A big favor.

"Sure, bro, what is it?"

I need to borrow some clothes and as much cash as you can get your hands on.

"What?"

I need to borrow some clothes and as much cash as you can get your hands on.

"Why?"

I have to… go away… for awhile… incognito.

"Why?"

No reason. I just do.

They whisper to each other for a few seconds and then Neil left to hit an ATM.

"I know you won't tell me what's going on, and that cool and all, but if you are really in trouble, you have got to let me know. I'll do whatever it takes for you, you know that, right?"

Yeah, I tell him, but this is all I need right now. We talk randomly until Neil gets back. I pack a bag full of Stephen's clothes and catch a cab to the airport.

36

In my defense, it's not really "stealing" when the owner tosses you the keys and stuffs a five dollar bill in your breast pocket while saying take good care of the vehicle, if you really intend to take good care of it.

Okay, so maybe Josh did misrepresent himself, but he never lied. He never said he was a valet. The guy just assumed that.

Like it's our fault the guy made a bad assumption. First syllable of *assume* makes it perfectly clear it's not my problem.

We're headed south on 295 like a bead of sweat trickling out of New Jersey's arm pit. We had tired of passive-aggressive fighting over what music to listen to so we agreed that whoever was driving can pick the radio station, as long as it's rock and roll. There's only so much country a guy can take before he must kill Josh. Fucking cowboy douchebag.

Josh is doing lines off an old road atlas and we were both sharing a rather poorly rolled joint that is dropping more hash than ash. It's been months since I smoked dope and this bullshit has me looking like a paperboy in his first rain storm.

I'm coughing, my eyes are watering, and I'm swerving into other lanes. This all seems pretty funny.

Not the whole being-on-the-run thing, but the driving part. That's what's funny.

Now the on-the-lamb thing? That's scaring me. My personal freedom is on a damn short fuse right now. By tomorrow, the cops will realize I'm gone. If they haven't already. Running is an admission of guilt and I may be guilty but I'm not guilty enough to run away like this and I don't deserve to beat down by some deputy assistant deputy sheriff like it's a Fraternal Order of Police initiation ceremony.

So I banged an underage runaway. Or two of them. It's not like I knew she was 16 and her leaving home shouldn't confront me any. Addresses are just for tax purposes any way. It's her life; it's her home she left. I'm not a social worker; I can't save anyone. If I knew any of them were underage, I wouldn't have slept with them. Ok, that's not exactly true. But I definitely wouldn't have let moron-boy sitting next to me videotape it all.

Just to be honest, the crime itself doesn't even bother me that much. I could feign remorse throughout a hearing, even a trial, but where's my heartfelt god damned motivation? End of the day, sex is a biological thing. You gotta have it, I just need it more than everyone else. Or from everyone else. Whatever. So it's not the crime; it's the time. Jail time. Ass raped by some strung out biker, knife in the back while trying to shower right there, shoving a Viagra down my throat so the new meat can suck me off time.

Without any warning, I slap Josh in the back of his head. He drops the joint, knocks over the road atlas, and squeals, "What the fuck? What the fuck was that for?"

If you have to ask, I'm not gonna tell you, I tell him.

I'm not gonna draw a map for you, I tell him.

Get bent, I tell him.

In total and complete silence, we drive down the road. A road sign tells us Philadelphia is 75 miles away. The city of brotherly love is just 75 miles away.

I'm not thinking Incestual Love but I can't blame you if you were.

Josh is more than a little pissed about the coke getting dumped on the floor. Even though it was, like, a line that got dumped. Well, just snort it out of the all-weather floor mats that haven't been vacuumed out since last winter, bitch.

Josh is getting all bent out of shape by this and calling me all sorts of names. Asshole. Motherfucker. Piece of flaming shit.

Peter pumper.

Waste of sperm and egg.

The ingrown hair on the pimple on the ass of a retarded mongoloid.

Asshole, he repeats earnestly.

Pillow-biter. Are we still talking about me?

There are all sorts of nature type things out the window. Trees and sky and birds and soft white clouds and unidentifiable road kill.

Not a cat, maybe a small dog or a groundhog. It's a medium range small furry mammal, that's all I can guarantee. Could've been two cats, I guess. Then there are water towers and power lines and diesel tankers and other things that aren't nature.

Man takes over nature. Man imposes his will. Manifest destiny. Man is the top of the food chain and nature had better learn to cope if it wanted a peaceful existence.

Right now, Josh's and my own peaceful existence has just been interrupted by a minor brush fire on the floor on the passenger side of the car.

Apparently, Josh never tried to retrieve the joint he'd dropped. The thought of picking up a flaming object off the carpet on the floor didn't seem to get through his skull.

And of course, he blames me.

■ ■ ■

Granted, pulled over on the side of the highway, smoke from a small fire caused by an illegal drug billowing out of the window was not the smoothest way to start our great escape. Granted, seeing a police car pull up behind us was the most depressing sight I've seen. Granted, there was half an ounce of cocaine sitting between us on the middle console. Please, Mr. Police Officer, ignore that sweet, sweet cocaine.

"What seems to be the problem, gentleman?"

Josh leans over me, pushing his hand a solid five inches north of comfortable on my inner thigh for support and says "Nothing, officer. I just dropped a cigarette and it sort of caught on fire. It's all under control. We were just about to leave."

"U-huh. License and registration, please. And proof of insurance."

Why not just ask for an autographed copy of the Bible?

Now, I'm a rather passive man. I don't cause much trouble (okay, outside of statutory rape and murder. And grand theft auto. Shut up.) and I've always been respectful towards cops. But this was different. This was impending arrest.

It was time for a new approach.

Ignoring the officer as if he wasn't a person, I turned to Josh, who was busy screwing around inside the glove compartment looking for documents and demanded, "Josh, what the fuck does he want? Get rid of him 'cause we need to be in Philly about twenty God damned minutes ago. Hurry this shit up." Josh just stared at me like a kid at his first strip club.

The cop shifted his stance a little and leaned in closer. I think one hand may have moved closer to his holster, but that could just be me. "Excuse me, sir. I'm going to need to see a valid driver's license, the registration to this vehicle, and proof that it is insured." Well, it seems Mr. Highway Fucking Patrol didn't like being ignored.

So I obliged him and sneered loudly in his face, "Actually, you need to get back in your little cop car back there and get the fuck out of my face."

"Sir, please step out of the car."

"Sir, please drop to your knees and suck me dry." If you are going to go down, you might as well keep swinging. Besides, this feels good in a Russian Roulette way.

He turned bright red. I was getting through to him. "You've until the count of five to get out of the car slowly and put both hands on the hood of your car or you'll have an abrupt introduction to my Taze-A-Tron."

"You know what? I consider that a threat. A threat. My taxes pay your fucking salary and you think you'll just resort to fucking Nazi scare tactics on me? Do you have a fucking clue as to who I might be?"

"Sir, I don't care who you are, you're going to jail."

Today would have been my three-year anniversary with Monica, by the way.

Josh looked like he might very well wet himself, but I was going to need his help to pull this off. "Josh, tell this man who I am." I pretend to find something of great interest in my finely manicured fingernails while Josh stammered out a response.

"Um...he's...well, he's John Sterling, sir."

"Indeed," I said, projecting the same calm, cool, and collected nature of the man who brought you *All Cousin Gang Bang Survivors*, despite the gun-toting law enforcement official looming outside the window. "John mother fucking Sterling. And John Sterling, TV star, needs to be in Philly as soon as humanly possible for a benefit for homeless kids or some other retarded shit. And I'd hate to have to say I was late because some cop had to prove a point."

I can see recognition pop into his yes and he immediately relaxed. "Ohmigod, my wife watches your show every day! Wow. You're a star. But I called the stop in. I have to check your license."

"No time. If you want an autograph, I can do that. But you trolling back to your car to spend half an hour running some background check on some broken down 90's era mobile modem to connect to a twenty year old government database of kiddie pee-pee touchers isn't going to work within my time constraints."

"Sir, Mr. Sterling, sir, I can arrest you if you resist."

"And I can say you threatened me and only arrested me for a high profile arrest. It's your career and you know I have great lawyers. Jesus, do you even shave? Is this your first week on the job?"

"I've been on the force for 4 months. Sir, I *need* your license."

"And I need you to get the fuck back in your car and get the fuck out of my face."

"Sir what is-"

"Am I not speaking English here? *Tu habla Espanol?* What gives? Are you brain damaged or something? Get back in your car and leave us the fuck alone. You are about to open a case of whup ass. Twenty-four cans of it. Now, really, are you ready for that? I can own you. I'll be your pimp and don't you ever forget it. I will have YOU on MY show. Want your wife to make an appearance as well? She'll LOVE it, though you probably won't. Now turn around and get back in your car, get on the radio and say everything is cool, you're going further down the road to run radar. Understand? Hello? Do. You. Understand?

The cop stood silently, probably contemplating a world well above his pay grade. Of money and fame. After a few seconds he turned towards his patrol car. Two steps later, he turned around and said, "Can I still have that autograph?"

I grabbed a piece of paper, signed John Sterling, and told him to hold on to it, the value would be skyrocketing in the next few days. With that, the cop got back into his car and we left.

■ ■ ■

Josh is staring at me. "Whoa man? Where did that come from?"

"Did you feel like going to jail?"

"Well, no."

"Did you feel like killing that cop?"

"Well, no."

"Then I was keeping us out of jail without having to kill a cop. Next time be more careful about the joints you drop."

We drove on, my heart was racing like a speed addict against my rib cage.

I'm not thinking Four Hits of Speed and a Lap Dance but I can't blame you if you were.

That whole state trooper thing was way too close for my taste. Probably way too close. Nothing is going to stop that cock monkey from running the plates on this car. We had to avoid that sort of stuff. Maybe back roads were going to be a better option. We had to stay away from cops, and they would know soon enough that we left south through Jersey. They are probably going to assume we'll cut west through Pennsylvania, unless they think we are heading south.

We could head back north, double them up. That would put them off the scent. Unless that cop doesn't report he pulled us over because he realizes he'll get in trouble for not checking my license and registration. But he did say he radioed in the stop.

I suppose heading east until we hit Portugal isn't much of an option here.

There's just too much going on, too much I have to think through. We pull into a Motel 6 to do some thinking and get some rest.

"Josh, go in and get a room."

"Why me? Why don't you get off your fat ass and get us a room. Emancipation Proclamation freed the slaves, man."

"First of all, the Emancipation Proclamation only freed the slaves in the Confederate states. Second, people recognize me and we don't need me recognized, now do we? So get in there and get us a damn room." Josh gives me that look a woman gives you when you ask for a blowjob and gets out of the car.

Fuck my life, I'm remembering a time when I couldn't get a blowjob on demand.

A few minutes later he returns with a key to room 215. We gather our bags and walk up the concrete stair to our room.

The room is powder blue, which is maybe the most sedate color for a room I've ever seen. This should be the room in a suicide crisis hospital for high risk cases. Josh says he was going to grab a shower. I plop down on my bed and turn on the TV to see what was going on.

Cheerleading on ESPN. Whoever calls that a sport needs a full-frontal lobotomy. Or they had one already. Click.

MTV is showing some reality show, which has about as much reality as a hummer from Giselle. Click.

I'm not watching the fucking Fuctkard Wives of Wherever. Click.

Reruns of Friends. Click.

Comedy Central is showing *Encino Man*. Funny, but I don't remember much comedy in that flick. Click.

The History Channel is blessing us with a narrative of the Boer War. Click.

CNN Headline News is showing... is showing... is showing... "Josh! JOSH! **JOSH!!!** Get out here now! We're on TV! We're on CNN! We're so fucked. Screwed. Right in the ass. Oh man."

Josh comes running out of the bathroom, towel around his waist, looking like he saw a ghost. "What? No way."

"...so now Metro Police are following the few leads they have as to the disappearance of John Sterling and his assistant Josh Embryo after..."

"Embryo? Your last name is Embryo?!?!?"

"Shut up, asshole."

"Why didn't you ever tell me that?"

"How do you work that into conversation? Here's your coffee, by the way, my last name is the same as a developing fetus. Asshole. Didn't you ever look at my paycheck or anything?"

"...they are believed to be tying to leave the country. Police have only said they are looking to speak to the pair in connection with multiple investigations. Today in Argentina, Prime Minister..."

Are we having fun yet?

37

At least now we know. It puts the nail in the escape unnoticed coffin though. We are officially suspects- fugitives- and they seem to have a firm grasp on our escape plan. They may not know we are shacked up in a Motel 6 but they seem pretty keen on our possible intent to leave the U.S. immediately.

Airports will be looking for us.

The border police probably have our pictures plastered all over the damn place. And we are nowhere near a border.

Wild West-style Dead or Alive posters are coming to a post office near you. We are going to be bigger than OJ and will probably trigger an Amber Alert. Wait. That's for kids. I mean Silver Alert? Right? Fuck it, it's a full-on rainbow alert with clown shoes and fucking balloons at this point. Our faces are already to be on billboards and telephone poles all over the east coast, all they need to do is add the FBI tip line phone number.

I briefly wonder if America's Most Wanted is on the air, and if so, I should call my mom and tell her to tape the episode

I am about to be on. Have her save some of my headlines. One day, we will look back on this day and laugh, right before a million fucking volts of electricity charge through my body and explode my fucking brain.

Maybe I'll get more press in the tabloids. TMZ is going ape shit, I'm sure.

From weatherman to talk show host to fugitive. From normalcy to the drug-laden alternate reality of fame and fortune to whatever this is. A fugue maybe? Or paranoid disillusionment coupled with delusions of grandeur. Even schizophrenia. Whatever. I consider scheduling an appointment with my old therapist but remember my life is totally fucked in a way he can't help on.

I am going to be the answer to a Trivial Pursuit question in about twenty years.

I can just see us hiking across the Canadian border, looking north towards the vast tundra, or crossing the Rio Grande in the wrong fucking direction and looking for a small cantina to lay low in.

This is turning into a Saturday Night Live sketch. This is the downward spiral. This is the abyss. This is the ninth circle of hell.

This is getting back everything I broadcast multifold. What thou reap so shall thou sow. Eye for an eye, one person's dignity for another's.

Whatever happened to "roll with the punches" or "turn the other cheek"? And who made karma the be-all-end-all? Fuck this balanced universe noise right now. Stephen Hawking can suck a fucking hard one.

No matter how biblical I wanted to look at this, it wasn't getting any better. Our plans were found out. The cat is out of the bag, after it shit in it. Every law enforcement agent in North America is looking for us and they all knew the easiest way out was crossing the border, be it on a plane, a boat, on foot, or through the air.

This is getting more worst-case-scenario with every passing second.

■ ■ ■

"Uhh, well, I guess, if they're going to uhh be watching for us to leave the country, then we don't leave the country. It's that simple, John."

Wonderful logic for a retard. I'm starting to worry about the water supply in Josh's hometown.

"So let's just drive into the country's interior," he says, gaining confidence in his plan. "The breadbasket. The amber waves of grain. Nebraska, Oklahoma, wherever. They would never think of that. Who's going to look for us in a fucking cow field?"

The FBI, mostly.

"So you want to drive into the center of the United States in hopes we can avoid United States police officers?" I wasn't exactly thrilled with this course of action but it was starting to make some sense to me. When you can't escape, hide. Disappear. Josh could evaporate any where, probably, just by growing a beard, wearing a ball cap, and driving a taxi around. But my face, it's pretty well known. You can show people our mug shots side by side, but eleven times out of ten, they are only seeing me.

"Sure. Why not? Got any better plans?"

Of course I don't, and it does sound better than either becoming a white rapper or putting speed in the drinks of senior citizens.

We drive on. We head west on Highway 30, which runs parallel to the Pennsylvania Turnpike for most of the way from Breezewood to Pittsburgh.

I am driving. Josh is shotgun.

A sign tells me that the local Chili's is responsible for maintaining the next 3 miles of the highway.

Unexpectedly, Josh asks,"So what's the weirdest thing you and a girl ever did?"

Huh? "What do you mean? Like weirdest place? Position? What?"

"I guess all of them. Give me a list."

"Dude, you sincerely need help."

Josh smiles brightly. "I'll take that as a compliment."

There's this bizarre duality to Josh. He can be hyper-functional and insanely focused yet at the same time, totally unable to process his own reality. Or it could more a two halves don't add up to a whole sort of thing.

"More proof. I'll need a minute."

"Fuck a minute. If I give you a good one, you'll be able to counter easily."

"What are you talking about?"

"Once, I gave a girl an Angry Dragon."

"What the hell is that? A wrestling move or some shit?"

"No, grandpa. We're talking about sex here." An Angry Dragon is when some chick's blowing you and, just as you know you're about to toss some babies, you smack her hard on the back of the head. She'll snarf your load and when she comes up, all pissed off and your cum dripping from her nose, she'll look just like an Angry Dragon.

How could you not laugh at something like that? "But won't she get pissed?"

"My God, yes, she gets pissed. All to hell. We're talking no pussy for weeks."

"Dude, that's rough."

Hardcore.

Slowly, my mind turned, opening files and memories searching for "crazy sex shit". The distraction was clearly working.

"I've had rodeo sex once."

"What's rodeo sex?"

This isn't something I'm proud of mind you. This was just a bad, bad joke. But it was college, I was drunk, and more than a little pissed at my then-girlfriend. It just sort of happened.

It's when you're getting a girl doggy style, and you start to get into it and then you call her sister's name or her mother's name or your ex's name. Hell, you could call her Mike, whatever gets her bucking. Then you just grab for dear life and try to hold on for 8 seconds. It's tough, trust me.

"You did that? John Sterling? John Sterling rode the hornless bull? Rodeo sex?"

Whatever kids are calling it these days. "Of course. 6 and a half seconds. And may I remind you that we're here right now because of my sexual deviancies and the fact that you were dumb enough to record them for prosperity?"

■ ■ ■

We are somewhere in Indiana on some winding back road. There's piles of hay and chickens and corn everywhere. We're talking American Gothic right here. Totally rustic.

"Did you know that a typical American eats over 1000 chickens in the course of their life?" Of all the random shit to know. You'd really want to know these things. First of all, how does Josh know this, and second, why does he feel the need to share?

And then I drive through this swarm of black insects, splattering them all over the windshield and all I can wonder is "do insects suffer?" When their little nine celled brains explode, do they worry about how their families will move forward? Is there that moment of recognition that it's all over? Is there an insectile philosophy, a light at the end of the tunnel?

And these motherfuckers are not wiping off. Their hairy, black, little bodies popped like tiny miniature rotten fucking cherries and you could not believe the amount of viscera there was in these bad boys.

I suppose insect blood is thick as it's just smearing around on the windshield.

Their wings and legs and abdomens were not only stuck in the blood smears, but in my wipers as well.

I must admit, I am quite impressed with the insects in Indiana.

Half hour later, I'm finishing up a joint and Josh is half asleep next to me. We're listening to this old Beatles mix CD Josh brought. Mostly Sgt. Peppers, some other stuff.

I've stopped pondering the fate of these bugs and rather savor the accomplishment of killing them. Each smear is an notch on my belt. I am ridding the world of this pestilence.

A dime a corpse would solve a lot of problems. Issues. Can you tell we are running low on cash by this point?

38

"But I have no idea how to dance," Josh insists. "I can't dance period. At all. There's not one dancing cell in my fucking body."

"Do you have any other great ideas about making some money? We've got less than a hundred dollars left. Do you think that's going to hold us up until the coast is clear? Well? Do you?"

Josh stares at me, gray eyes tying to drill through me with sullen rage and hatred.

"Plus, if you're going to be a stripper, you do have the whole coke thing going for you. That's a bonus."

"How do you even know they need a dancer? And even if they do, how do you know they'll want me?"

I remind him that we're in North Bumblefuck and these places are always hungry for fresh meat.

I'm not thinking Mad Cow Disease but I can't blame you if you were.

"You know, John, you are such a prick. A god damned cock smoker. You know that? Fine, I'll go in there and whore myself for you, my fucking pimp. I'll embarrass myself so you can make money."

"But Josh," I tell him, "you'll probably like it. All those women, shouting at you, fighting over each other to shove money down your g-string. It's quite the ego rush."

"Oh, you think I'll like it? Yeah right. It's humiliating as all hell."

"I'll bet you $ 50.00 you like it." Josh looks at me askew, then agrees.

So what do I tell the manager, he asks.

"The truth."

"That I'm on the run for murder and statutory rape?" Stupidity like this should really be painful.

"No, idiot boy. Tell him you were driving across the country with a friend and you ran out of money. I'm sure they hear it all the time. Just walk in, give the manager your story, shake you love maker, snort a few lines and just fucking do it."

"You know, if you weren't a famous TV star, you'd be doing this."

"If I wasn't a TV star," I remind him, "we wouldn't be in this position."

I agree to pick him up at 2:00 am if he's not back in 15 minutes. He gets out of the car slowly and walks dejectedly into the club. Twenty minutes pass and then I drive away.

Serves Josh right. First he exploited the women, now they get to exploit him.

Oh, irony just abounds in humanity.

■ ■ ■

I had fallen asleep in the car waiting for Josh to get out of the club. Really, I have no clue what time it is when Josh knocks on the window of the car. I let him in and the shit-eating grin he has on spoke volumes.

"That was, without a doubt, the best evening of my life. It was amazing. Look, I made almost $350! In cash! This kicks ass, bro! Looks like I owe you fifty. Mikey, he's the owner, he wants me to stay for the weekend. He even knows the guy who runs the Hoosier Inn down the road, and we're getting a room half price. The perks of adult entertainment, huh?"

"That's great," I told him, "just wonderful. Now point to the hotel."

"But don't you want to hear about it? I was dressed as Zorro. They de-haired my chest- feel this." He grabs my hand and goes to put it up his shirt.

"There's no fucking way I'm feeling you up. Leave me alone, I'm tired."

"But this lady gave me $50 to run her finger through my butt crack. $50."

"So we're paying for the hotel with butt crack money. Who cares?"

But there is no stopping Josh when he has a story to tell. He tells me all about the free (though subpar) cocaine, the oil they used to greased him up, the envious looks from lesser looking strippers, the catty locker room talk.

He tells me about the soft cups they had to wear to protect their packages so they couldn't get hurt by the occasional client. At least they let you look bigger. They come in circumcised and uncircumcised. Nice.

He tells about the shower he took in front of thirty middle aged women, about the thong underwear he wore.

He reveals himself as a true master of the trade by telling me the secret was to pretend the audience was your girlfriend. Just how often do you dance in front of your 38 girlfriends?

He says the lighting in there dries out your skin and you have to put moisturizers on after every session. Don't forget about the special gel they use to keep your nipples hard the whole time.

Now he's talking about his thigh waxing.

I'm not thinking Too Much Information but I can't blame you if you were.

He rambles on until we finally arrive at the run down, shit pile hotel. He goes for the keys while I get our bags out of the trunk.

The room has a dank, yellow and pastel theme. It's the sort of place where a grown man would play Dungeons and Dragons for hours on end while making up conspiracy theories about the Jews, Kim Kardashian, NAMBLA, and the New York Yankees. Really.

I fall asleep while Josh watch reruns of *MASH*.

I have strange dreams that night. Since the pills ran out, I'm having dreams again. Dreams of Monica trying to seduce me.

I missed you, honey. I missed you a lot. You know what I wanna do. I wanna be your little hump puppy.

Then we're having sex in my old middle school cafeteria while all the people from The Five O'Clock News watch, shouting out advice and giving scores. I'm pretty sure there's a clown there too, but I can't be sure.

As disturbing as the dreams are, waking up is far, far worse.

Josh is in his black thong looking thing, dancing in front of the mirror. I let out a shriek and pull the covers over my head.

"Hey, John, do you think it looks sexier when I do this, or this?"

"How would I know, I'm not looking. And I'm not going to. I'd probably turn into stone or something."

"Well, how the hell am I going to get good at this if I don't get feedback? Remember, those tips are our whole income."

Hyper-focused Josh is back apparently.

This is like the time my college girlfriend did a study on how many times a 20-year-old male could ejaculate in twenty-four hours. Minus the fun or orgasms.

"So, is it better when I run my fingers under the waistband, or when I run them over my crotch?"

How am I supposed to know this, I ask him? I'm not a desperate, middle aged, divorced woman with 12 cats at home and every issue of *People* since the Carter administration.

"Sex is just sex, man. Think of me as a woman. Tell me what you want momma to do."

This is only going to get worse so I tell him, "I don't know, but I always liked it when a girl touched herself, so I'd go with that."

I have to take a shower now, I am dirty.

■ ■ ■

I am in the middle of my shower when I hear Josh banging on the door. I ignore him, instead focusing on lathering my scalp with the complimentary shampoo that comes in a tiny plastic tube.

He keeps banging on the door.

I keep ignoring him.

He's hitting the door so hard, I can see it bending from the frame at the top and bottom.

I keep ignoring the bastard.

Finally, I turn the shower off and yell, "What?"

"Don't use all the hot water, man. I'm going to need some, too."

"Why don't you just shower at your oh-so-sacred club tonight?"

"Yeah, I will, but this bronzer says it works best when applied after a hot soak. It opens up the pores or some shit. It says right here. 'Best Results After Hot Soak.' It's in black and white, man. You gotta do it."

"Screw you, Josh. So what if you don't look bright fucking orange tonight? This isn't a career or anything. It's a fucking Joe-job to pay the bills." He's taking this sense of commitment a little too far if you ask me.

Shampoo suds are getting in my eyes and I am still standing naked in the middle of a moldy shower. Pimp life, for sure.

"Sue me if I want to look good for my customers. I'm sorry I care."

"OK, whatever, Christ. Look, order a pizza and I'll be out in a few minutes. I have to rinse off and shave, OK?"

"Cool. With pepperoni, right?" Yeah. Sure. Whatever.

I manage to not cut myself when shaving, which is practically a miracle considering the generic disposable razor I am using. It has a deep blue color and only one blade. There was no smooth glide strip. I hate disposable razors like I hate fucking kids. As soon as I get some cash I'm going to buy one of those forty dollar razor jobs that have the razor cartridges five for, like, eight bucks. Every swipe is like seven blades, a rough up with pumice and a clear-coat moisturizer backfill. That's just what I want. Maybe that Shave Club thing.

As soon as I open the door, Josh, uncircumcised dick and all, is squeezing by me to get in. The first thing he does is complain about my hair in the drain. The first thing I do is ignore him.

I throw on an old pair of shorts, clicked on the TV and flipped to CNN Headline News. I am a regular on the Entertainment Roundup. This right here, me in this room right now, this is entertainment.

It isn't long until my face pops up. Today, authorities say, I remain a fugitive, on the run from the law. Chances are good, authorities say, that I remain in the country, hiding out. It is very unlikely, authorities say, that I left the country as of yet, though it remains a possibility they are willing to face.

This 24 hour news cycle has mindless speculation down to a fucking science. There's no new information. No additional facts. But they will keep you on the end of your seat regurgitating the same conclusions you would have come to by yourself. Just say they haven't caught me yet, you fuckers. Stop reminding people to think about me, damn it!

Even better, after continued harassing from various magazines and news shows that she do an interview, Monica has done an interview with Cosmo wherein she tells all that our marriage fell apart for "sexual" reasons and that I was always a little reserved.

No mention of pornography, mind you.

Nope, I was the pervert here. The deviant. The closet case. The freak. The dirty old man.

She tells Cosmo that our sex life was "trite" and "repetitive." That I was only into "standard" positions and lacked "imagination." Sorry I'm not into nine-ways. I soon learn from Fox News or CNN or I don't even know anymore that her pornography career is being heralded as a triumph for modern feminism. This is definitely CNN territory. So yippee for women's rights. Freedom, liberation, no bras, ten dudes at once. How the holy hell did I become the bad guy here?

And of course the pizza guy shows up while my picture is on the screen with a large red "WANTED" across it.

"That'll be $13.48. Man, they still haven't caught him yet?" I'm face down counting money. "I heard he's in France with his 15 year old boyfriend. Hope they catch him soon."

"Yeah, so he can get what's coming. Keep the change. Later."

Where in the world did that boyfriend thing come from? I'm not gay. I never experimented in college when I was drunk. No anonymous blowjobs in the bathrooms at the airport. And pedophilia isn't my cup of tea. I never even looked at the Olsen twins, I swear.

I'm straight and the world thinks I'm dating a 15-year-old French boy.

I tell Josh about what I saw and all he wants to know was if he was mentioned.

"No, Josh, you weren't the TV star, remember?" He looks at me blankly with a touch of hatred in his eyes.

"Don't be surprised if I'm dead when you get back from stripping," I say.

"You're not going to kill yourself, you'll be at work. I got you a job at the club."

"I can't work a job, retard, remember? People will see me. I'm John fucking Sterling."

"Oh, don't worry about that, no one will see you at all. That's a key part of this job."

39

"A cum cleaner? You want me to be a god damn cum cleaner? There's no fucking way in the world I'm going to clean up cum all night."

"If you can wipe your own ass, you can do this job. You walk in, spray disinfectant, run a paper towel over it and toss it. Repeat as needed. They give you rubber gloves so you are protected from the AIDS." The AIDS, he tells me.

"Oh, and people won't recognize John Sterling is cleaning up their ejaculated semen?"

"Of course not. People don't see the cum cleaner. They don't want to, it embarrasses them. That's the whole point."

I'm not thinking The Sociology Of The Public Masturbator but I can't blame you if you were.

"If it's a male strip club, why are guys jerking off," I asked him.

He tells me there is a traditional club attached in the rear. It's a smaller stage and less busy, but it doesn't take much to get the crowd riled up. Plus, there are the homosexuals for the guy side. Even though it's the Midwest, there're still plenty of gays. Not to mention all the repressed latent homos, he tells me. He looks me straight in the eyes when he says scientists have proven that everyone has at least something gay about them. I wonder if Josh The Unstoppable won't be satisfied until the whole world is jerking off in male strip clubs.

Josh breaks it down for me. People go into private booths with a twenty-one inch TV and watched any of the different channels.

Interracial blowjobs on Channel One.

Threesomes on Channel Three, foursomes on Channel Four. Makes sense. More than four would probably lead to issues with character development.

The messy facial cumshots on Channel Seven while Tight Anal is Channel Forty-Seven. Fatties on Channel Twenty-Seven. Asian Lesbians on Channel Nineteen. Miss Piss is non-stop on Channel Eight.

You don't even want to hear about fetish Channels Thirty through Thirty-Six.

Gay themed channels are from Channel Fifty-Two to Seventy One.

Bestiality was on Channel Forty-One and Forty-Two. German Hardcore your scene? Then check out Channel Eleven. Dutch Hardcore? Flip to Channel Twelve.

The men whip it out and pull a Pee Wee. They shoot their load and leave. The cum cleaner, me, goes in and cleans it up.

"And you get 25% of the take from the booths. Mikey knows he makes bank there, the quicker you clean them, the quicker the next guy can spank it. On weekends, they make between $500 to $750. That's a pretty penny for you."

And all I have to do is clean up jizz. I went to college for this?

We're driving to the club a little after dinner and Josh is still talking, about how much he likes stripping, how it's his dream job.

The glamour. The money.

The women fawning over him.

The bright lights and the free coke. He always mentions the free coke but has stopped mentioning it's below standard.

All I can think about is his "career" as a white rapper and laugh to myself.

"OK, when we get there, I'm taking you to Cameron. He's, like, 70 or something and blind as a bat, so he won't know who you are. He'll tell you what's up and everything."

A decided resignation hangs over me as I enter the club. From a famed talk show host to cleaning up semen from a nudie booth in some random dive strip joint in Indiana.

New low- I could officially be a guest on my show.

Cameron was clearly as old as Josh indicated. He had me follow him to an old janitors closet and pointed at a bucket.

"That's yours. Everything you need is in there. Gloves, spray, towels. This ain't brain surgery, kid, don't go screwing the pooch tonight."

I try hard not to screw pooches, but one can never tell. It's been one of those years.

"You sit here. You watch this box. When a light turns from green to red, that means someone in the booth has left. It's like the confession booths at church. You go to church, boy? Give them a quick minute so they're good and gone, then just go in and clean it up. When you're done, you come back here, flip this switch, it lets Dorothy know it's clean, and wait for another. Just keep doing it."

Ah, enlightenment, oh sweet nirvana.

Now *Come As You Are* is stuck in my head.

"Now, most guys do it on the floor or wall. Locate the stain on the floor or wall and spray. I usually spray once, then spray one more time. Don't forget the gloves, things can get sticky. A few guys go on the screen, sick bastards. Make extra sure the screen is always clean. That's the key here, a clean screen. You listening? That's important. You have to look out for the guys who try to rub the stain in with their feet. Makes it hard to see, and by then it's all ground in and hard to get out. A real pain in the arse, if you get me. If that happens, spray it with Tilex. Sounds weird but it works. You got all this or should I write it down for you?"

■ ■ ■

I was a cum cleaner for three days. There is something a bit transcendent about the job, a grand pattern to it, a flow that gives you a deep sense of accomplishment. Making sure that you left the chrome shining bright, the TV screen clear and not a trace of pre-ejaculatory lubrication anywhere.

Really now, I just cleaned up strange guys' loads.

And these guys were strange. I had to kick out one guy who kept "accidentally" walking in on guys. It happened, like, ten times. Then there was the guy who requested an unclean cubicle.

Another guy who just rolls the dice as to where the guy before dropped his gob, go in, and spanks it. This is how he gets his kicks.

I caught a guy who was going in to a booth after some one left it to lick up the evidence. Then there's the ongoing problem of people trying to sneak others in with them, forcing me to go over and knock on the door and say 'One at a time please.'

I saw more guys with obvious boners and their zippers down, running to get more change than I'd like to admit.

Then there's an entire sub-category people who got off by leaving their door open slightly so others could see them flog-ging the dolphin.

And people cum in the weirdest places, too.

On the door, on the seat, on the far wall, on the TV. Once I went into a booth and it was dripping from the ceiling, eight feet high. That guy had to throw it up there or something. That or he hasn't blown his load in a few years.

Trust me, there wasn't a square inch of this room that wasn't either chrome or plastic. Everything could be instantly cleaned. Every night we sprayed them down with hot water.

But the booths made money, so I made money. Three nights of cum cleaning netted me almost $600 while Josh made just over $2000 between Thursday and Saturday. We had plenty of money, the gas tank was full, there was plenty of junk food and Josh picked up an ounce of dope from one of the bouncers.

So, in retrospect, no I didn't think going into some mom and pop convenience store was going to get me charged with another murder.

Yeah, well, hindsight is twenty-twenty, right?

40

It's just one of those average normal looking thank-you-come-again type of stores. The sign reads "Hoosier Market." Does everything in Indiana use Hoosier in its name or is this just me?

I walk in behind Josh and head to the back of the store to grab a Mountain Dew twenty ouncer. My sunglasses are dark and my cap is low. Josh is debating on what flavor of iced tea is right for him.

Earl grey or raspberry? Diet or just sugar free? As long as he stays away from the energy drinks and male enhancement products, I'm in a good place.

Just as I pick up a bag of Doritos, we hear a shout from up front.

"This is a hold up." For fuck's sake, thieves in bum fuck Egypt.

"Put your hands over your head." Seriously?

"Give me the fucking money before I blow your head off." Totally not what we need right now.

"You two back there, get your asses up here now."

I learned young to do whatever a person with a gun tells you to do something, you do. Unless it's a Jersey state trooper. As we are walking up front, Josh hands me money.

"What's this for?"

"It's the fifty I owe you for stripping, remember?" Christ, he's retarded. In his mind, he's probably settling up old debts, while that little brain bouncing around in his skull drifts off to la la land. Detached Josh is back, it seems.

The robber sees this transaction and demands our money as well. Strike one for Josh.

The attendant is struggling with the safe and the robber is looking increasingly antsy. He has a sawed-off shotgun and plenty of tattoos. He's dressed entirely in black but I doubt he's a big fan of the Cure or anything.

The attendant is now sweating profusely and still hasn't opened the safe. The robber's incessant waving of the gun in front of him didn't help matters much.

The robber puts the gun up to my chest and tells the attendant that if the safe wasn't open in one minute I am going to be spread about the store in various bloody chunks.

Great, and me wearing dirty boxers. Guess Mom was right after all.

When he starts the final ten second countdown, Josh decides to intervene.

"You can't shoot him, he's John Sterling." Strike two for Josh.

The robber looks at me hard and lowers the gun.

"Yeah," continues Josh, "if you killed him, you'll be railed. He's famous."

Before the pros and cons of celebrity status can be discussed further, the attendant opens the safe and places a stack of money on the counter. While the robber is putting the money in an old gym bag, Josh asks the attendant if he could keep quiet on the fact we were here. He explains the whole situation with the kid and he agrees. Then Josh turned to me and remarks how it would be funny if the cops thought we did the robbery.

Strike three, Josh, you're motherfucking out.

The robber must have connected the same dots and we jump as a shotgun blast tears through the store. Both barrels discharge at once and the attendant's body is blown back a good five feet, slamming into the pornography and rolling papers behind the counter. Then the robber tosses the empty gun to me, which I stupidly catch, and then runs out with the money.

"What do we do," I asked Josh. "What now?"

"Well, is he dead?" Yeah, Josh, two shotgun blasts to the chest at three feet usually proves fatal.

"Should we call the cops?"

Oh sure. Hi, police? I'm a wanted fugitive and I just witnessed a murder. While only my prints are on the gun, I didn't do it. I swear, honest injun. No, I have no witnesses that can back up my story, at least none that aren't wanted felons. Oh yeah, there's also some narcotics in our stolen car.

"No, I'm going to pass on the cops, Josh."

So we do what we do best. We run.

■ ■ ■

We are ten miles down the road before Josh decides to say anything. I was silently driving down the road. It was a beautiful day. Was. Note the tense.

"At least there isn't much blood on us."

Yeah, but it doesn't seem all that comforting given that the rest of it isn't exactly in the kid anymore either.

"Evidence to get rid of, I mean." Suddenly I'm reminded of Josh's uncanny ability to get rid of evidence.

"It's obvious to me," I say, "that we turn ourselves in. Next town, we find the police station and turn our sorry asses in. This has gone on way too long now."

"There's no way we can turn ourselves in. Not after we killed that guy."

"What the hell? We didn't kill that guy, Josh. I was just buying Doritos for fuck's sake."

"That's not how it will seem. How will it look to the cops? To the media? We're as good as convicted already."

For the first time in this whole running-from-the-law thing, Josh is right. Damn, I hate to admit that.

We try to figure out our next move. We know we need to get off the roads quick. The cops will have wall to wall roadblocks across the state when word gets out we killed the guy. We can't get a hotel room, because our faces are probably being faxed to every hotel in the tri-state area. We're fenced in and the noose is getting tighter.

Basically, we're fucked in the ass. Without any lubrication.

Dry 'til you die, motherfucker.

It's ok, I'm getting used to it by now. I wouldn't know what to do if I wasn't being shit on. I've adjusted to my environment.

So Josh decided all we need is somebody to get the hotel room for us.

Someone who doesn't have a problem breaking the law. Someone who does things for money.

He's so totally talking about a hooker.

"Haven't we broken enough laws by now? Two counts of murder, let's see, there's also rape, and those drug charges. Now you want to add solicitation of prostitution? Great."

Of course, we have no other alternative. It's a sad state of affairs when you need to hire a hooker just to get a hotel room. In high school, you just had to pay somebody's big brother a case of beer.

And, as usual, I can't be the one to hire our little walker of the night, Josh had to do it. That means no proper vetting. That means a roll of the dice whether Josh The Unstoppable or Josh The Dim is doing the talking. We park outside some crappy bar near the highway and Josh checked his hair in the mirror.

"Wait here", he tells me and walks inside.

I wait for almost an hour. Finally he comes back with some thirty-ish looking woman, opens the back door and gets in behind her.

I guess you don't find good looking whores in dive bars in rural Indiana.

She gives me directions to the "inn", turn here, past this, park next to that. She gets out and comes back with keys. We follow her up the stairs and into the room.

I toss my stuff on the far bed and lay down, almost forgetting she's even there.

She starts unbuttoning her blouse, incapable of reading the room.

Josh explains that we didn't want sex. Well, I wanted sex, but not from her, and Josh's assertion that everyone has a little gay in them made me think a threesome might end poorly. Anyway, we just needed her to get the room, he explains.

"You don't at least want head, hon? It's my specialty, after all. The best knob polish in Jefferson County. Just don't cum in my mouth unless you're wearing a rubber."

That's fine, I'll pass. Not today.

"What, you guys fags or something? That's cool. I never done a threeway with homos before." And after tonight, you still won't have.

No, we're straight, good night.

"No, no, it's cool. I like faggots; they're nice."

"Look, lady, my boyfriend is in France right now, OK?" It just sorta comes out like that. I'm tired, I'm frustrated, and current events are short circuiting logic at this point.

Her face lights up as she realizes who I am. Famous. Wanted. John Sterling. World-class idiot.

"You're wanted for rape or something, right? I saw you on 20/20 or something, I think. Maybe 60 minutes."

No I'm not. No you didn't. And we both know you don't watch 60 Minutes. No one under 60 does, especially trashy rural Indiana whores.

"Sure I did. Dianne Sawyer warned me about you."

She's missing the point here.

"Look at my driver's license. It says William Meridan! See? I'm not him."

Still missing the point.

"Look, here's $50 to prove I'm not John Sterling and here's another $50 to prove you didn't see me."

This will not go down in history as a well spent hundred dollars, let me tell you.

41

I wish that I could say that our capture was dramatic. A car chase, a shoot-out, a hostage negotiation, six naked chicks and so much white powder that DEA and Homeland Security had to be called, anything. Instead, instead it comes down to three cops pounding through our hotel door while Josh and I lay in our beds watching a rerun of *Mr. Ed*.

They are really polite to us, too.

They made sure the handcuffs aren't too tight. They guide our heads down when we get into the back of the squad car. Two of them even ask for autographs.

Josh is pissed, but in a way, I am relieved. Whatever solace this brings me is quickly crushed by the realization that now I have to deal with Prison Josh, a man determined to rehash all the little things that went wrong.

Should have stayed on the highway.

Should have kept stripping.

Shouldn't have dropped that shotgun.

Shouldn't have hired that hooker.

I point out that maybe we shouldn't have laced anybody's water. Shouldn't have videotaped sex with minors. Shouldn't have snorted lines off an underage girl's ample bosom.

There are plenty of legal women we could have snorted that coke off of.

Shouldn't have run away. That was the big one right there, running away.

I am brought into a bright interrogation room with an obvious one-way mirror and two cops, one with a notepad and the other with a cup of steaming coffee. The first cop offers me a cup, which I decline, and then goes about perusing some papers that are spread out on the table. I assume Josh is in a similar room with similar cops and a similar mirror and papers on a similar table.

"So tell us about the robbery. Start at the beginning."

"It wasn't a robbery," I explained. "Well, at least not by us. Some other guy wasted the attendant. We were just buying Doritos."

"Then why are your prints all over the murder weapon?"

"Because the guy tossed the gun at me after he shot the attendant."

"And why weren't his prints on the weapon?"

"Because he had gloves on." Am I the only one who could figure that out?

"Mmmhhmmmmm," smirks the cop to himself as he scribbles a few notes.

"If I was planning a robbery, I would wear gloves," I insist in an attempt to cram some knowledge into his skull. "The fact I left prints lets you know I didn't do it. I'm not an idiot.

I'm not that fucking dumb. I don't even know how to fire a shotgun."

"How did you know a shotgun was used in the commission of the crime?"

"Because I was a witness to both the robbery and the murder. I was so fucking close I had to throw my shirt away because Tide only guarantees *stain* removal, not *brain* removal." Apparently common sense isn't a requisite to work as a cop in Indiana.

"We recovered said shirt, by the way." Thanks for the FYI, dude. I wonder offhandedly which unit is responsible for sifting through the trash for evidence, and what the success rate is. How many dumpsters do you need to dive through to find a solid piece of evidence?

"If you witnessed such a crime, why not call it in?"

Is this the point where I plead the fifth? Or is it drink a fifth? One of them stops me from incriminating myself. Unsure, I opt to just stare back.

"Ease up on him," the other cop says, "he's answering our questions unrepresented."

"I don't know," says the cop, "you seem to have a criminal history. New York wants to talk to you about another murder that took place prior to your fugitive status. And there's some narcotics charges waiting back east as well. What part of that *doesn't* make you a prime suspect?"

Come on, there had to be a camera in the store somewhere," I pleaded. That would prove my innocence. Cameras-judge, jury, and exonerator. FACT.

And it would have helped, too, if it were working. Apparently it broke a few months back and the owner was too damn cheap to fix it.

I'm not thinking Worthless Miser but I can't blame you if you were.

This goes on for another hour or so. The first cop tells me the sentence for aggravated murder in Indiana could be death. But don't worry, says number two. More than half of the white inmates on death row get killed by prisoners before the state could get around to it. That's quite the relief. I'd much rather be killed by a homemade knife made out of a bedspring than the painless fashion in which the state disposed of its prisoners.

They ask me again if I want a lawyer. Again I say I don't need one, I am innocent. Guilty people need lawyers. I'm not guilty.

Well, not of this crime anyway.

I don't bother to mention that I will be lawyering-so-the-fuck-up when I get back East, the judge will need to sit on a stack of phone books to feel like he's still in control of his courtroom.

Finally they tire of all this and I am escorted back to my cell. Josh is waiting for me when I got there. He is sitting on his bunk, head in his hands.

"Man, we're so screwed. We got to bust out of here before we get killed."

I'm beginning to think that Josh may actually be a retard.

I remind him that we didn't kill that guy, that we were totally innocent of that crime. Indiana doesn't have a thing on us. It's the other charges that have the distinct potential to turn our asses into currency spent on cigarettes and nudie magazines. Besides, the mere fact that we were being kept in the same cell points to them knowing they don't have anything on us.

He told me that his cop told him they have three witnesses that all said they saw me pull the trigger while Josh was emptying the cash register. They told him that he would be in as much trouble as me for the murder. He was the accomplice and would be punished the same.

Was I even aware of the punishment?

"Hell yeah, but we'd be killed by a rapist first," I tell him. "Trust me."

■ ■ ■

I don't have to tell you that the mattresses in jail are rock hard. I mean, I am used to the crappy, semen soaked bed rolls in all those trailer trash inns, but this is like sleeping on concrete. A cold, lifeless concrete that reminds you that you are behind bars, a ward of the state.

Sometime around when the sun comes out, an officer clangs something across the bars, says good morning, and slid two trays of food under the bars for us.

"What the hell is this?" demands Josh, who sounds likes he's been up for awhile and isn't happy about it.

"It's your breakfast, moron. Eggs and bacon, slice of toast. Orange juice and water." The guy looks like he may be missing a chromosome or something.

"I can't eat this trash. Bacon is swine. I'm Jewish. Bring me something else!"

At the exact same time, the officer and I said, "You're a Jew?"

"Yes, I'm a Jew. Is there something wrong with being a member of one of the oldest religions in the world?"

The officer looked quite befuddled by all this. He shakes his head, wipes his brow and said, "But you ain't looking Jewish."

You would have thought he told Josh that he had a fifteen-year-old boyfriend in France or something.

"I don't look Jewish? I don't *look* Jewish? What, I don't have a hook nose? I'm not lending money or stealing your children? I'm not shooting it out with Palestinians? I don't look like a kike to you? What, I don't look like I could have survived the Holocaust? Where's your god damn supervisor, you profiling ass fuck."

I'm not thinking Overreaction but I can't blame you if you were.

"Christ, sorry man, I didn't mean it like that. I'll get you some oatmeal then. Geez." He takes Josh's tray back and goes to get the oatmeal.

"Josh, I don't think he meant it like that. Seriously, man, I didn't think you were Jewish either."

"Yeah, well, you never asked, now did you?"

"No, but I didn't realize Embryo was a Jewish name."

"Oh, so if I was named Goldstein you would have put it all together? Besides, my name is Joshua, you freakatard."

"Well, I would have maybe thought you were Jewish if you were named Goldstein. It's not like you wear a beanie on your head or a Star of David pin on your lapel or something."

Anti-Semite he calls me.

Discriminator he calls me.

Gentile piece of shit he calls me.

A bunch of words in Yiddish he calls me. I don't even want to know.

The guard brings Josh a bowl of steaming oatmeal and he keeps calling me names.

Hate filled bastard he calls me.

Cock smoker.

He just keeps going and going with this.

He reminds me of the First Amendment. The freedom of religion.

I'm not thinking Masada Complex but I can't blame you if you were.

He mutters more Yiddish into his bowl of oatmeal and complains that it's too lumpy. It's too hot. There's not enough flavor. Where's the syrup? Maybe if he loved the Virgin Mary the oatmeal would be more suitable he tells me.

I hate Prison Josh.

42

The routine goes something like this- wake up with the sun because, of course, our window faces east with a wonderful, unobstructed view. Next we eat a crappy breakfast with shitty coffee, and more interrogation with the same moron cops. These guys are either slow or enjoy hearing the same story time after time after time. Then, lunch by myself in a small closet-looking room with a small black and white TV that only gets PBS.

I know more about the mating habits of the dung beetle than I'd like to admit.

In the afternoons, I to sit and listen to the DA tell me my story right back to me as if I wasn't the one who told the cops what happened. Next, I am put back into my cell and Josh usually appears about an hour or so later. I cannot overstate how much I look forward to that hour of solitude. Finally, we were allowed thirty minutes of "exercise" in a caged area outside that is easily smaller than my college dorm room.

All of this leads up to our dinner. Every night, we get the same dinner. A slab of grey meat that was obviously a work-horse at one point but has been so heavily processed it could probably be certified vegan at this point, and what is either mashed potatoes or creamed corn, and two slices of bread with a tiny pat of butter. Oh yeah, and a glass of water with four ice cubes in it.

Every time, four damn ice cubes. There must be a law say-ing prisoners get four ice cubes with their water at dinner.

Not three.

Not five.

It might provoke a riot and no one wants that.

Then we sit in our cell until we fall asleep. Which shouldn't have been too bad, but Josh always jerks off as soon as he thinks I am asleep. There's no easy way to tell your cellmate you're still awake once he begins to pleasure himself.

And I don't even want to think where he's shooting his load even though I bet I could clean it up.

This goes on for three straight days. We never see any oth-er prisoners, we never see any other police officers, nor do we do anything different. Then, on our fourth day of captivity, things change.

Instead of individual interrogation, we are both brought into the same room, a much bigger one with eight men in there, the DA, my two cops and five people I had never seen before in my life. They sit Josh and I down and wait. And wait. Just staring and I have no earthly idea for what. Five minutes went by in total and complete silence. Josh cracks first.

"Is there something we can do for you gentlemen? You want to see what's under the uniform or are we here for a reason?"

The DA looks at Josh with at tilted head and replied, "Well, looks like we have good news and we have bad news. Good news first. Looks like you didn't kill that kid. We ran tests on your shirt and there were only minor traces of gunpowder on it suggesting you were five to seven feet away from the weapon when it was fired. Also, a witness came forth and said she was outside the store when the murder took place and you didn't pull the trigger. Looks like you're innocent."

Josh and I exchange sighs of relief. "So what's the bad news then?"

"Well, New York has petitioned for both of your extraditions on many charges, including murder in the third degree, statutory rape in the second, and possession of a controlled substance. There's also a car theft charge in there as well."

Yeah, forgot about that one.

"Look, Mr. Sterling…"

"My actual name is William Meridan, you know."

"I know, but we all know you as John Sterling. Big fans of the show, by the way."

Nods of agreement around the room.

"Any way, we hate those big city liberal motherfuckers but laws are laws and we have to do it. There ain't nothing we can do to prevent what's about to happen. We're going to do you a solid and delay your transfer as long as possible to pull the hairs on their asses, but we can only stall so long. By next week, you'll be in their custody."

Great, and we actually *did* commit those crimes. Nothing like an impending conviction to ruin your day.

"Well, could you just let us escape? Leave our cell unlocked tonight and we'll just disappear out of sight?" Oblivious Josh, the eternal optimist, makes an appearance, ladies and gentlemen.

"Not in the cards, amigo. Despite what they may think, calling us up and talking all slow-like, we're still professionals. Nope. You're going back to New York to face charges. Sorry, but do the crime, do the time. Can't help on that. But I tell you what. This is America, boys, and in America, everyone gets their day in court."

We are taken back to our cell and talk about our options. If we are going to end up there anyway, why fight it? It was inevitable and unavoidable.

"But maybe we can escape," Josh mused.

No fucking way. Why add to our charges? It's time to face the music.

■ ■ ■

Four days later, we are on a plane headed for LaGuardia Airport. We land on a private runway and are escorted out by our armed guards. We are then whisked away in the back of a huge black up-armored SUV and taken immediately to what would be our home for the foreseeable future.

That night we are given separate cells. They inform me that Josh and I won't be able to communicate with each other until the trial was over. Like we wouldn't have already worked out our story if we were going to use one.

It's obvious that New York cares much more for their high-profile prisoners than Indiana. My bed is slightly cushy, my meals are both edible and different every day, and I get cable TV, though the channels are limited.

I get ESPN, but there's no ESPN2.

No MTV, PBS or Comedy Central. No Fox, but I get Fox Family.

No NETFLIX or Hulu either.

The next day, I meet with my agent, Kyle, and he introduces me to the head of the of lawyers he's hired. Some big shot named Jennings Cloude Patterson, III. I could just call him JC.

JC assures me that I can tell him any- and everything. He doesn't give a fuck about dead grannies or gang banging 16 year olds or any of that bullshit. His sole job is to clear my name. Morals, he promises me, are a trivial weakness in his profession. I look at my agent and he is nodding his head furiously so I play along.

JC asks me to explain in great detail what happened. I tell him. Yes, I did have the drugs, yes, it was me in the video with the girls, yes, I knew about the speed in the water, yes, we stole the car, but no, I didn't know she was underage, no, I didn't steal the car, Josh did, and no, I didn't plan to use the speed. I found out after it was too late.

"Well, don't even fret over the drug charge. Celebrities do drugs, people know that. Hell, they'd be pissed if you didn't do coke. Plus, it was found in your place of business which could be accessed by scores of people. Actual possession has not been determined."

America's War on Drugs at it's finest, folks.

He flips through his notes. "Yeah, and the rape thing is no big deal. She was consenting, right? She misrepresented herself to gain access to a star. As a guest on your show, it'll be no issue to showcase her character, or the lack thereof. It's no big deal. At worst it's just a slap on the wrist. I'm confident they will drop those charges."

I'm not thinking Lady Justice Is Blind but I can't blame you if were.

"Same with the car thing," he continues. "Christ, car thieves get less time than jaywalkers. Now... this murder thing. That's going to be a harder nut to crack. Anyone else know about this plan?"

"Just Josh."

"Well then, we need to find out what his story is going to be. If it matches yours, they won't be able to get you for murder, that's for sure. Now, you rest up. In two days, you go before the grand jury. Trust me, they'll be taking this to trial but it's still a formality." JC gets up, shakes my hand and departs, leaving me with Kyle.

"So, how have you been, John?"

How the hell do you think I've been? I'm sitting in jail with a laundry list of charges.

"Oh, you know. Can't complain."

I've been fired from the show, he tells me. But with all the hype surrounding my manhunt, *TalkShowX* has become even bigger business. It has just sold into syndication netting me a cool seven million dollars. Crime does pay, he tells me.

Guess that's how I'll pay JC and his team.

Three book companies have offered me big bucks to write my life story. A&E is in production for *John Sterling: The Man and The Fall*. I'm going to be played by a cast member from *Beverly Hills, 90210* but they won't tell me which one. I'm voting Jason Priestly, but Luke Perry would be OK, I suppose.

Wal-Mart has pulled my line of action figures but now they have some sort of cult status. Some are going for triple digits on Ebay. There are apparently dorm rooms across the country with shrines to John Sterling. A bootleg of the now famous underage-girls-and-coke video can be downloaded in the right, seedy corners of the internet.

"Is there anything else you need," my agent asks me.

Just a swift kick to the groin.

43

Grand jury proceedings are a joke. They lasted fifteen minutes before the judge decides this bad boy is going to trial. The next day, on the advice of both Kyle and JC, I enter a plea of guilty on the charges of possession of a controlled substance, deteriorating the morals of a minor in the second, conspiracy to facilitate grand theft, evading arrest, and reckless endangerment in the third. Josh is charged with the same things, but his is plain old grand theft, and he is hit with manslaughter in the second. He also pleads innocent. What a dumb ass. Note that a team of bulldog lawyers is above his paygrade.

After the first day of the trial, the DA offers me a plea bargain. Time served, 500 hours community service, and three years probation. JC tells me it is a good deal. I mull it over and figure it'd be a terrible waste of the taxpayer's dollars to keep dragging this out. I graciously accept the offer that keeps me from being ass-raped and gang-shanked in prison, with the minor provision that it's not binding until a verdict has been rendered for Josh.

Josh, on the other hand, thinks it's dumb to back down from his trial and fires his lawyer.

This is his show now. His spotlight. He's not the assistant here. He's the talk show host now. Sort of.

Think of it as stripping in a legal sense.

He declines further counsel and decides to represent himself. In his opening remarks, he rambles about the great media conspiracy against him. The biased press coverage, he tells the jurors, focuses on conjecture and suspicion, that they peddle petty conspiracy theories as facts, all to avoid having to show he's quite innocent. Again and again, Josh attacks the media. The press only serve to drive the point that he's guilty when, in fact, he's quite innocent.

It's more of the same for the various witnesses called to the stand. Josh questions them- the judge calls this "leading"- and ultimately puts on a big show of how innocent he is.

He's innocent as a baby asleep in its mother's arms.

More innocent than George Washington and his cherry tree. I'm pretty sure Josh wasn't very good in history class.

More innocent than a pussy by the side of the road. Yes, he really used that word instead of cat.

The judges overrules him every time, even threatening him with contempt five or six times. Josh just keeps chugging through though.

The judge is at his wit's end but the jury remains hung. It's probably less that Josh's arguments are anything but sane and more that the prosecution seems to have an issue calling credible witnesses and producing evidence.

On day two, Josh calls the officers from Indiana to the stand and rips into their blatantly racist treatment of him while he was in their custody.

How they tried to force feed him pork.

How they mocked his last name.

How they told him he couldn't survive the Holocaust. Man, does he ever drop some huge puppy dog eyes on the jury when he delivers this one.

The trail that day lasted five and a half hours. The next day, six hours.

On day three, a bomb drops that shocks the world.

■ ■ ■

The judge has just told Josh that he'd be held in contempt if he didn't settle down for what looks to be the last time. His face is bright, bright red but that doesn't matter to Josh. Josh instead counterpunches, taking a page from Hollywood and telling the judge that *he* is going to hold *him* in contempt. I check my watch. Good, I should be out of here by lunchtime.

At once, a bunch of suits explode through the door, Kyle and JC leading the storm. I mouth a silent "what the fuck?" at them but they are focused on the judge.

Seems, someone confessed to doping grandma's drink.

I slink down in my seat and keep my eyes down. I know for a fact that Josh had done it. Hell, even if he hadn't told me in advance, this trial by itself is more than enough to prove his guilt.

But, no. Apparently, one of those KKK bikers had confessed to juicing the poor woman. He'd been brought in on completely unrelated charges and during interrogation, spilled the beans. Yeah, sure, I know he only did it for attention, notoriety, a little more pull in whatever prison he's heading for. But now, every camera in America was in his face for trying to frame a star. No. THE star, John Sterling.

The details of us fleeing, statutory raping, snorting just seem to melt away after that. Overnight we go from suspects to victims, and victims are gods in America. My net worth skyrockets as everyone is heads over heels to be the first to apologize. Be the first to tell me they knew I was innocent all along. The first to capitalize. The book. The movie. The website. The charity. The blowjobs.

Let me tell you. That first mouth hug outside of the criminal justice system is glorious. It's like that movie where the 80 year old man is magically transformed into a vibrant 18 year old boy who can fire his load like a cannon.

What I'm saying is, she was dangerously close to choking and drowning simultaneously. Oh man. I'm still thinking about it.

All charges are cleared for me but Josh gets slapped with 1000 hours community service, and 90 days in county jail minus time served. It's less the grand theft charge that stuck and more the pissed off judge who sentenced him.

I visit him once a week. I ask him if he's someone's bitch yet and he gave me this weird look. I guess there are some things you don't really want to know anyway.

My head is still spinning after this five ticket ride at Disney World and I decide to spend some time recovering with Stephen and his...um...husband, I guess. My mom comes over a lot and it was nice to see my family, even Neil. Every couple of days, Kyle checks up on me, promising something big as soon as I'm ready.

I'm not thinking Vultures At The Carcass but I can't blame you if you were.

I tell him to hold that thought. I needed to recharge myself. I need to be William Meridan again. John Sterling is dead. R.I.P.

Nowadays, I'm happy to just be in Stephen and Neil's guest bedroom and watch the History Channel and maybe read some old science fiction novels. Sometimes, I talk to Josh about the show. Sometimes, we talk about how big it could have gotten.

But I don't really think about it much anymore. When I look back at it, it's sort of embarrassing. All this trouble, it's pretty obvious to me now, was brought on because of sex and drugs. I'm not saying either is bad, mind you. But it can't control your life. I was so concerned with getting head after the show that I didn't care that the show was a horrid cancer.

It's not entertainment, it's avoidance. It's about making your life better by watching these jackasses on stage. You can forget you prematurely ejaculate if you see five guys who can't even get it up. Their problem is worse than yours, so yours disappears for that hour.

Your girlfriend may have cheated on you, but at least it wasn't with your brother.

You may want your ex-husband back, but you're not willing to strip on national TV to get him.

No matter how bad your life is, these people are worse.

44

It takes a little over a month before I'm ready to discuss Kyle's big offer. Cryptically, he tells me to watch *Meet the Press* on Sunday. I think I remember my dad watching that when I was a kid, but I never took an interest in it myself.

Turns out its an election year. Some gray-haired dude is talking about making a difference, compromises, being non-partisan yadda yadda. It's boring. I don't care about these issues. That's for other people to worry about. I just pay my taxes and expect my trash to get picked up and some war in the Middle East to be funded. It's just a popularity contest manifested on people's greed and how well someone can give a speech. Hell, having a zero in the "experience" column would probably score me half a vote.

And that's when the gray-haired dude drops my name.

William Meridan.

"It's time for a fundamental change in our government," he tells the host. "We need a change and it will come in the form of grassroots changes at the local and state levels. A name that can... no, WILL, lead this change is William Meridan."

What.

The.

Actual.

Fuck is going on here?

The gray-haired guy is going on and on and I can't really follow what's being said any more and my cell rings and it's Kyle.

"I told you it was big news."

"Yeah, big news. But politics? I don't know the first damn thing about politics, and I don't fucking care to learn."

My head is still reeling and I feel a little bit dizzy. Neil walks into the living room, sees me swaying a bit with my eyes glazed and asks, "are you okay?"

Holding my cell phone out towards him, I say, "This motherfucker wants me to jump into politics. Politics."

"I'm not sure that would be a good idea."

"Exactly!" I put my cell to my ear and say, "why in the world would you think I'd want to be a politician? I'm seriously re-evaluating you as my agent, Kyle."

He says a bunch of things that don't really register with me. I'm about to hang up when he tells me to meet him for lunch tomorrow.

■ ■ ■

That night, I'm talking this fucktarded idea over with Stephen and Neil. Stephen loves the idea. I think the idea to him though, is "famous brother". Neil, on the other hand, is more skeptical.

"It sounds like they are trying to exploit you."

"That's what I said."

"They don't have a platform, man. That just *sounds* sketchy. Did you end up in this situation before- out of a job because of a scandal?"

"That's also what I said." I always thought Neil was a level-headed guy.

The debate rages on. This is like sitting in a staff meeting for *TalkShowX* when the producers are debating whether or not a show would cross the line.

Film *Strippers With Down's Syndrome* or not.

Air *So What If I'm Pregnant, I Wanna Do Heroin* or not.

Become a politician or not.

I'm not thinking To Be Or Not To Be but I can't blame you if you were.

Shit. We filmed and aired both of those. Son of a bitch.

Stephen and Neil are getting pretty heated over this. I'd never seen them have an argument, and frankly, this was a pretty stupid thing to fight over.

"He's being taken advantage of, and it's for political gain. That's just un-American."

"There's nothing more God-fearing American than public service."

"God has nothing to do with it."

"It's a freaking phrase, an idiom."

"You're an idiom that ends in –T." At this point they are both standing up and the tone of their voice has sharpened.

"Namecalling. Namecalling, Neil. That's real mature."

"Whatever. You are practically asking your brother to whore himself out when he hasn't recovered from the last freaking time that happened." Neil is dropping the lame F-Bomb. Weaksauce.

My brother steps closer to Neil. "Come on, this is an opportunity to heal thyself while healing others too."

Neil inches closer to Stephen. "Did you ever think it might be time to put someone else's good before your own?" His eyes have the fire in them. You know. *That* fire. Oh good Lord, they are going to fuck or fight. This isn't Sublime, and it's most certainly not all the same.

"This is self-therapy, though. Cleanse the soul through good deeds. Karma. Maybe you just don't get that the needs of the *many* are more important than the needs of *you*."

"There's no me here. It's about your brother."

"Then maybe you should butt out of family business."

"He's my brother in law, this is my family business."

Stephen turns bright red at the flaw in his argument and goes on the defensive and it sort of knifehanding Neil telling him that he knows what he meant, but he has a bottle of Gatorade and it's splashing all of the place.

"How do you drink that shit? It looks disgusting." Neil makes a disapproving face.

"Huh? It's Gatorade Frost. Stop with the change of topic."

"Frost? It looks like semen."

"Oh yeah? Then I'll think about you while I drink it," Stephen retorts.

I just threw up in my soul.

45

The next afternoon, my mother calls. She'd been calling the last few days, since *Meet the Press*, but I just wasn't up for whatever she had to say. I can only delay the inevitable for so long so I begrudgingly answer.

"Why on Earth wouldn't you tell me you were running for office?"

"Mostly because I didn't know I was."

"Don't you lie to me. They said your name on *Meet the Press* and you had no idea. Poppycock."

I try to work up the motivation to explain the situation to her but there's no point. Sitting here, in my brother's house, being offered the chance to run for office is giving me a healthy dose of ennui.

"I'm not sure if I'm going to do it. I'm not ready for the public eye yet. I may never be. I just want a quiet life. I have no need to work or anything."

She sighs and I know she just rolled her eyes.

"Why don't you want to do it?" Your Honor, a leading question.

"I don't want a stressful job, I don't want to be in the public eye, I don't want to be a politician. These people, the Millennium or whatever guys, they don't even know what they stand for. It's like being in a band with no gigs or a baseball team that doesn't play games. What's the point?"

"What did your father, rest his soul, do for a living?"

Where the hell is she going here?

"He was an actuary. He crunched numbers. Flexible accounting, he called it, I think."

"And do you think he liked doing that?"

"Yeah, I guess. That seems the type of thing you'd only do if you liked it." Unlike, say, cum cleaning.

"He didn't. He loathed it. Every day. His father would only pay for school if he took business classes, and back then, there weren't scholarships all over the place."

I'm a horrible son, but I'm thinking when my mom's last gangbang was.

"So he got his degree but do you know what he minored in?"

Of course I have no idea what my father minored in. Honestly, I wasn't even sure they had minors back then.

"Poli-sci. He was really into political science. He went to anti-war rallies. Equal rights demonstrations. He wanted to change the world for the better. He wanted to help people."

"Okay, so dad was one of those change the world types. That was him."

"Yes, it was, and it was what I loved about him. His passion." Please, don't mention passion, mom. Not about dad. "He was motivated to help others. Right wrongs. Leave a mark."

He left a mark on a certain religious store, but there's nei-ther here nor there.

"Good of him," I tell her, "but then why didn't he?"

"Well, you were born. Rallies didn't pay. Sure, he could have blown his... *our* savings on mounting some campaign against someone with experience, but he had mouths to feed."

Guilt trip inbound.

"That's great, mom, but I'm not him."

"That's true, dear, but you are a lot like him."

"Mom, I'm just not up to this. Not yet. These last almost four years have been crazy. Porn fiancé. Mass shootings. Drug binges. Crazy, crazy sex. On the run. It's nuts and I just want it to stop. I'm tired, frankly."

"When your father died, I thought that too. We just had these busy lives and I wanted a break." Gag me. Ugh.

"But slowing down was really stopping. You can't stop."

Oh, fuck my life, that makes sense.

"Alright, dad was a young visionary. Was he a Young Republican or a doe-eyed Democrat?"

"Neither. He didn't like parties. He said that when you gave allegiance to a party, you lost your individuality."

"So he was a third party guy?"

"I don't think so but we didn't really have that back then. I do know that he aways said parties are pointless, it's the people that matter."

She's getting this distant tone, the kind she has when she gets wistful, but really doesn't happen much unless you are discuss a vineyard that shut down.

"I'll be honest, William. He probably told me millions of time, but really, when he got on those rants, got all worked up, I stopped hearing him. Not in a bad way. But I paid attention to his passion. His deep blue eyes and his strong voice. It was mesmerizing. I may not remember the message, but I will never forget the messenger. I so truly loved that messenger."

I could tell she was silently crying.

"William," she says, "you need to do what's right for you. But don't be scared, and don't ever, EVER, slow down."

I agreed to stop by on Sunday for dinner, and she hangs up.

■ ■ ■

I arrive at the restaurant and see Kyle seated with the gray-haired from TV yesterday. As I sit down, my agent says, "I thought we agreed on 1 PM?"

"Yeah. Huh. Well, my phone has been ringing non-fucking-stop since yesterday so I turned it off, and I wanted to clear the eight million emails I received over the last 24 hours out of my inbox. Couldn't you have told me this was what you were working on?"

The gray-haired man smiles at me and answers, "Well, you would have said no."

I'm not thinking Captain Obvious but I can't blame you if I were.

"My name is Jacob Strillington, and I represent the true party of the American people, of liberty and freedom, the Millennium Party, and I'd like to talk to you about not only becoming a member, but also an elected representative."

I try really, really hard to maintain eye contact with him, as if we are having an actual serious discussion. Still, that's a big no-can-do, brother.

"Politics aren't for me."

"That's why politics *is* for you."

No. No fucking Jedi mind tricks.

"Politics aren't for me, and I'm not for politics."

"That is exactly why you are for politics."

He explains to me that America is fed up with career politicians. They want change, but most importantly, they want to trust. He tells me I have that accessibility that allows them to trust easily. They can relate. And I'm thinking, sure, but as a talk show host. That's hardly a qualification for politics.

"The reality is," he calmly tells me, "you have star power."

"See, I've heard this before. That's how I got into the talk show racket. Look at how that worked out for me."

"Non-issue."

I have to wonder how being an ex-fugitive doesn't matter, and if that's the case, what the fuck does this party even stand for?

"So what's your platform?"

"We don't really have one. We are working to establish a logo first, then we'll worry about the product."

"That sounds retarded."

Before he can respond, my agent cuts in. "Will, this is the perfect chance to mold the party to your beliefs. You can be Moses leading the Israelites through the desert."

Josh would lose his shit over that comment.

"I don't want to be a political Moses. That's my whole fucking point. Am I stuttering or something?"

"Mr. Meridan," Strillington practically whispers, "just think it over. That's all I'm asking."

So that's what I do. Think it over. I spend the next fews days, practically in a haze, going back and forth on the idea. I wanted to stay out of the limelight but I knew that would get old quick. My entire adult life was in full public view. My most intimate details are on Wikipedia. It doesn't take an advanced Google search to see videos of my almost-wife getting gang banged. This is all I know.

And while this, if done correctly, would be the moral opposite of *TalkShowX* . This could almost atone for *Strippers With Down Syndrome*. Instead of making them feel better about themselves, I could just make things better. Granted, I know exactly nothing about the political process. I assume there is one. There has to be, right?

It's not like I care about the Millennium Party, which we all know will be referred to as the Willennium Party if I win an election and those memes practically write themselves. But if the people don't like me, then they won't vote for me. Right? It's a self-correcting system. And I'm not doing anything dishonest or immoral. If the opposition wants to put up a ton of videos of me flashing my pearly whites as some girl's head gyrates in front of me, and that bothers them, then they won't vote for me. So simple.

I'm not thinking A Caveman Could Do It but I can't blame you if you were.

So, at the end of the day, I have nothing to lose here. Yet, something way back in my mind tells me that eleven times out of ten, people watching that video are seeing my smile and not the girl giving me a blowjob. They'll see John Sterling. They'll see William Meridan. They'll see the man they fell in love with and who got them through those rough times. The man wrongfully accused by the corrupt, biased media. Exonerated and reborn to be a champion of the people. They'll be a room full of dudes at a bachelor party awkwardly watching the guest of honor's fiancé get triple teamed. The homicidal chick shooting up her own wedding reception in my name. The rookie cop breaking protocol in order to score an autograph.

Strillington has this all wrong. I don't have star power.

I've got god damned twisted steel wrapped in barbed wire sex appeal.

Charisma.

That unspoken mojo.

I am the art of making friends and lovingly abusing them. In a good way.

It's not like I'm a bad person. I'm not. I may have done some bad things but with good intentions. I suppose I *did* like the path to Hell. But I'm not a bad person.

But my mother's words still echo in my damned ears.

I pick up my cell and dial Kyle.

"Call Strillington and tell him I'm in."

~~~THE END~~~

ABOUT THE AUTHOR

Tom Kuhar is a graduate of Rutgers University. He currently lives in the American Southwest and works as an analyst for a large, faceless corporation. He is married and has two sons. He plays more video games than an adult should, and he assuredly does not like long walks on the beach.

He can be reached at his website:

https://tomkuharwriting.com
or email:
tomkuharwriter@gmail.com

ACKNOWLEDGMENTS

This book would never have been written without the constant support of Kamran Nowroozi ("dude, I've got three new pages…"). I owe a debt to William Nugent, who not only assisted with editing but helped hone the voice of William and especially Josh. Speaking of editing, Kevin Bloom wasted countless hours reading a book he probably didn't like, providing professional feedback and guidance, all because years ago I spent fifteen minutes helping him with something I pretty much had to do any way. Props to Matt Morgan who likely compounded his PTSD assisting with the editing process but oh well, dude. Also, thanks to Mark Douglas and Dan Huerter for the last polish applied this. I also need to thank my parents, who always made sure I had books to read growing up. Maybe giving me all of Stephen King's books when I was twelve wasn't the greatest parenting move ever, but it sure sparked a love of reading, which turned into a love of writing. Finally, my wife, who has been almost entirely supportive (she knows what she didn't do…) and got me my quiet time when I need it to do some work. Love ya, babe!

www.ingramcontent.com/pod-product-compliance
Lightning Source LLC
Chambersburg PA
CBHW022144170626
46807CB00005B/2062